THE WITCH'S FATE

USA TODAY BESTSELLING AUTHOR
WILLOW WINTERS

There is no path that you're on today that you have to be on tomorrow.
Everything can change, if only you wish, and that's a beautiful thing.

Dedicated to my therapist Paula for keeping me sane... mostly.

Happy reading loves...with spells and spice, you are in for a treat!

$\mathcal{S}$ome say it's dreadful, but I love my life.

My days in the meadow usually take on a similar shape. In the summertime, I rise early in the morning because the land rises early. The song of the birds is my wake-up call. That's the best time of day to tend my garden beds. Weeding in the heat of the afternoon is asking to become ill from too much sun, even if you *do* have magic. The morning sun is much better.

When I'm finished, I might walk to the small pond at the edge of the forest closest to my house and bathe. Then I have a bite to eat and bake bread, and finish any work left from the day before. With a flick of my hand the pages turn, and I read a bit in the warmth of the sun. Though I've already read my small collection of books many times over, a new book every so often comes my way and I enjoy the studies as much as the adventures. New spells come to me, and I refine them as much as I can before I write them down for anyone else to see. My grimoire is full of scribbles, but the papers I submit are proper and complete. Although I substitute some concoctions so no one may reverse the much-needed remedies.

My magic is powerful and yet, so often, I feel at peace in the quiet and lonesome. I look forward to long days of a gentle breeze and a divine sunset.

It's not quite summer yet, but it has been a warm spring, and I look forward to what is coming…no matter how unfortunate others claim my life to be. They know not of what a sanctuary it has become, they know only of why the powerful witch lives by herself and why no others join me.

There is almost no chill in the wind anymore as I go about my late spring routine, yearning for more warmth and the life it brings. Soon it will be high summer, with the crickets singing in the grasses of the field and late sunsets and those early, early mornings.

In the wintertime, I go to see if I've received any letters when the suns are highest. I don't care for the cold much but thankfully the winter is the shortest of seasons where I reside. Now, in the spring, I wait until the warmest part of the day is fading into late afternoon before I cross the field to the box where letters manifest themselves. A courier from the closest village leaves mail for me in a faraway land. A spell I cast years ago allows the letters to find themselves here. They call me a recluse, but I consider myself careful. After what happened, I take no risks, and my life is all I've ever wanted…mostly.

The ground beneath my feet is warm as I cross the field barefoot. The tall grass tickles my ankles and my thin linen dress drags behind me. Surely it will be dirty at its hem from the travels, but I love the way it feels, the way the wind blows back the sheer material. It reminds me of other times when I danced with my sisters under the full moon. Sisters who are no more.

When I'm tending to the gardens, I wear a straw hat to hide from the rays, but I take it off and let it swing from my fingers on my walk. A simple flick and the hat twirls beside me following the path I gave it.

The box is at the edge where the field meets the trees. A crossroads was needed, and nature provided it for me only a mile or so from my cottage. It's near the path that leads to the clearing but not across it. My house *is* visible from this part of the path, but only at a distance, and if you're not looking, you probably won't notice. No one ventures here though. Not for years. Not since my request to Chamberlain Colson. I'm grateful it was granted, but had it not been, I would have cast a shadow and hid there.

I turn my back on that small glimpse of my home, its thatched roof, wisteria growing up the side of the chimney, and light blue shutters accenting a dark blue door, and then approach the letter box. Even from a distance, the Canterbury bells and roses are visible, and if I focus and allow the noise to quiet beside me, I can vaguely scent the florals. Sweet and light and providing a decadence most do not know they should wish for.

The box itself is sturdy, made of thick planks and four logs with a door in the upper half wide enough to fit the rare parcel that might come and not much else. It took me weeks to build it, the magic was particular for such a long-distance physical manifestation. Still I cast protective spells whenever I think of it.

The wooden door opens with a faint creak, and I peer inside, my heart skipping a beat.

There are three letters inside. Chills run down

my arm and I know not why. My breath catches as if it is meaningful. Hesitantly, I pick them from the box.

Two of them are on cheap parchment—the kind any manner of people could acquire. Those who send wishes for me to aid them with magic and spells usually reuse each sheet and send letters on a narrow strip of parchment, and two of the letters are just that.

The third—

Well, I doubt it is a letter at all, unless it's a letter regarding something very important, simply because of the envelope.

The envelope is made of thick, creamy paper. There is a certain sheen to it even in the dim letter box. It has a smudge or two from being handled but still appears expensive and thoughtful. From here, I can see the ornate script writing on the front, though I can't read it.

I straighten up and look in every direction around me. As far down the path as I can see. Across the field to my house. All around, then again.

There's no one there, although I cannot shake this feeling about me. Memories of a different time flicker in the back of my mind. A time when letters such as this did not bring about so much unease. A time when laughter joined the songs of the birds in the early morning. A time much different from this.

Yet now, though I cannot hear anyone nearby enough to see me, I feel watched. I feel as though someone might be lying in wait to see how I react to the sight of this envelope. What would they get out of such information? What would they get out of knowing that I blinked at it, then blinked again, then finally double-checked to make sure the woods around me were empty?

Closing my eyes, I envision a bright white light encircling my home, growing broader and broader, encompassing the field, the path, and where I stand now. I whisper, "I wish to be left in peace." The light is pure; it protects me and there are no obstructions. Letting out a breath, I invite the calm air to soothe what has come over me.

There is only me. Myself and the letter—which seems to be growing larger by the second.

With a final jerk of my hand, I pull out the envelope.

The writing on the front is elegant calligraphy, and my name is much smaller than the words that announce who it is from.

This must be an invitation. The calligraphy

announces that this was sent from Prince Adom and Princess Charlotte.

I close the letter box and move back out of the trees, slipping the letters into the cream linen pocket purse tied around my waist. It's slightly darker than the dress I wear, which is long and has wide sleeves that drape down my wrist. Nervously, I play with the hem as I venture back home. The invitation drags toward the earth, weighing me down. I know I cannot possibly be made to walk slower by a single envelope, but it certainly feels that way.

I focus my attention on the land around me as I cross the meadow, my dress brushing over the tops of new spring wildflowers and grasses that have already grown tall from the spring rains.

My cottage sits alone in a dip of the meadow on the other side from the letter box—not too close to the trees, but not so far from them that it feels too exposed.

Like me, the cottage is alone. For company, it has my small well and outdoor oven and the firepit, as well as my garden plots. I added a small bench last summer. Although I believe I've only sat on it once and no one sat beside me. I merely enjoy the idea of company and the aesthetic of such things so that those who have passed and yet have not passed may feel welcomed.

I detour to the garden beds, putting the invitation firmly out of my mind for the moment.

One power I've developed so well I barely have to try to conceptualize is growing edibles from a seed with ease. Fruits and vegetables, whether from bushes, plants or trees. It is no bother. At the closest garden bed, I kneel at the side of the tilled soil and brush my fingers over it, searching for the presence of seeds hidden below. It's been some time since I've tended this section.

It's only a few moments before I find a seed, its life and future concentrated in a tiny patch in the earth.

Then I close my eyes and imagine setting that life free from its small vessel. I imagine what the seed—the small piece of the whole, in this case—will become.

What it will become is a sweet potato. I feel it growing under my fingers, pushing the soil around it as it grows, until finally I can stick my fingers into the soft dirt and pull it out. The soil falls delicately, revealing the plump morsel for me to take.

That is the feeling of life. Of sustenance. It will do nicely for my supper.

Once I've brushed the dirt from the potato, I head inside. A bird calls as I pull open the door and enter; my gaze takes a few moments to adjust to the dimmer light inside.

The cottage is made up of only two separate rooms—the main room, and a small bathing room. However, the main room is large enough to house a coven of several members, especially if a few of those members prefer to sleep under the stars or in hammocks or on mats on the floor. What once was settles uneasily in my chest, and I close the door behind me.

After it was only me here, I turned the spare beds into other uses. I could not stand to look at the emptiness, so now my bed is the only one in the cottage. It's tucked in the far corner, a beautiful quilt and plush pillows lay over it. The makeshift bedroom is divided from the rest of the room by a low half-wall. My kitchen is on the other end, separated by another half-wall, and between is the rest of my cozy space. A blue velvet chair with embroidered florals on the back sits in the nook that consists of stacks and stacks of books. Plants in glass vases of all colors and finely painted porcelain pots line every window sill. From mint to dill and of course rosemary and lavender. The scents mix so heavenly.

It is quiet in my home. It is always quiet. So much as it can be.

Peace is why I live here—why I stay alone, in my solitary cottage, with no one else.

For a moment, a small moment, I envision bursting through the door to share the invitation with my coven. They would have taken the fine envelope from my hands and passed it around, leaning their heads close together to look at the writing and to test the thickness of the paper. I can hear the clucking of a sister's tongue as if she were still here. Their ghosts are merely memories, and I cannot bring them back.

But such invitations—such changes—never bring peace. If they did, I would not be here, well away from other people. In the last few years, I have missed many events and declined many opportunities to change my life once again. I cannot risk what happened happening again.

My heart races at the thought, though there's nothing in the cottage itself to worry me. If anyone remembers me—aside from Prince Adom, whose household has sent this invitation—they likely wonder why I have withdrawn from all others. I've heard the whispers that my solitude has turned to a tale children use in an attempt to startle one another. Some powerful witch alone in the woods… such a dreadful scary thing, I suppose, if told with a malicious tone.

Unless, of course, they all know what happened to my coven. In every land.

I do not withdraw to isolate myself. I withdraw to *protect* myself.

I am the only member of my coven remaining. I do not wish to become part of something else. It is too much agony to lose people like that, and I will be happy if it never happens again in my lifetime.

And so I have not gone to the Convergence Games, the contest held in the capital city—a battle to the death.

I have not gone to the United Nations meeting that takes place every three years.

I know of all these events. Even if I do not speak to anyone of them, the news comes in the letters people send to my letter box. There are mentions here and there of what is happening in the wider world. I read them with little interest and forget about them until the next one comes.

Whenever an invitation comes, I decline. If there is an event I *must* attend, I go in secrecy, disguised to hide my identity. This is the way of human witches. We do not trust other beings. I will never trust other beings again. I cannot remember the last time I ventured away. No, the contact I have is the one I'm most comfortable with: others needing my aid for magic. The spell to cast for a loved one or a tincture for a sickness medicine fails to remedy. That is where my comfort lies. Letters of pleas and wants from those I will never know apart from their script.

If I thought we could have peace, then I might have already tried to find a new community.

But I do not. The war brews on and I stay in my quiet place, helping where I can and living my life without causing harm and without being harmed.

With the memories racing in the back of my mind, I stare down at the invitation.

As it stands, I cannot take the risk. The invitation falls to the old wooden desk, my worktable that houses oils and crystals and salts that work in both spell jars and recipes, as I softly sigh.

I prepare the potato for dinner and spread out the other letters on a clean section of the worktable. This is how I make a living—by casting spells for others. They write their requests to me on parchment, and I send them back a spell or recipe for a tincture. With the money they pay me, I buy rare goods and delectables to live my version of luxury. It is a pleasure to coax spells from the earth and provide for others less fortunate.

It is a quiet life, but it is a life, and it is mine.

The invitation seems to stare at me from its place on the worktable, daring me to open it.

It does not matter what the letter inside says. I will not go. Even if it will be safe, which cannot be guaranteed, I do not know how I would bear being among all those people without my coven.

I write out two spells in response to the letters I received, then check them over. A love spell, my most popular request, and a protection spell, which is the strongest spell I can cast. I will take them to the letter box tomorrow with the others I worked on this morning, each folded in my signature pattern so that the recipients will recognize it. A wax seal and a hint of honey in the paper adds a special touch. They like it when I do this. More than one person has told me so, and that brings me a bit of satisfaction as well.

Happiness can be found in such small things, I have learned. And I am grateful for every small bit of it.

When the sun has finally set, I throw open the windows of the cottage, breathe in the fragrant night air, and search the dark sky for the moon.

Stars twinkle overhead. The trees in the distance sway in the gentle night wind. This is the most beautiful night I have seen in months. The warmth in the meadow has finally reached the point where it does not fade away overnight. I can smell new flowers and the earth around me awakening.

I try to tell myself that spring is still my favorite time of year, as it used to be in what feels like a different lifetime. That I can still feel the possibility in the warm breeze and hope, that's what spring brings most of— hope. But most nights, I do not feel such things. I feel my life stretching out before me, so quiet and so long. I *hope* to live a long time. I hope to carry the memory of my coven with me for as long as I can.

But the thought of all those years can be so lonely when the thing I see most—and seek most—is the many faces of the moon.

I am a moon witch, after all. I follow the moon that does not wish to chase. The largest moon. There are thirteen moons and two suns in our sky. The moons chase the mother sun and daughter sun in the sky, trying to get the daughter sun to win her favor.

My dedication to Dytnus, the eleventh moon and the witch's moon, is the source of my power.

With the moon shining down tonight in a sliver of a crescent, I light several candles around the cottage, black wax and white, and at last pick up the invitation from my worktable. I held it before, but the fine parchment is still a surprise the second time. The elegant envelope opens to reveal a letter written on the same fine parchment.

I was right. It *is* an invitation. The wedding of Prince Adom and Princess Charlotte will be held in two months' time. That is quite close, as far as these things go. Eight weeks. It will be here in the blink of an eye.

I read the words over twice more, a painful longing in my heart. It is a great honor to receive any letters from Prince Adom and his royal household. It is an even greater honor to be invited to his wedding to Princess Charlotte.

But I will not attend as I've already decided. Swallowing thickly, I choose not to acknowledge the longing that looms in my chest. I will send my regrets along with my other letters. I will not watch the prince and princess look deeply into each other's eyes and promise a lifetime of love and honor.

Yet I cannot bring myself to put down the invitation and take up my pen to write my answer.

I read it over again as if there will be something

new this time, then put it back in the envelope. I take it back out again, thinking I might need it to write my reply.

I wish one of my sisters was here to talk to me. I wish they were not to be silent forever in an afterlife I cannot reach. I do not know why it is nearly as painful to think of this cottage rotting into the ground and the meadow going silent, too, all of us forgotten.

Should I attend the wedding?

No. That is a fool's errand. It is not only dangerous, it will not bring me joy. Only pain lies beyond the veil of protection here.

I'm still holding the letter, reading it over in the light of the moon and my candles, when a long howl rings out from the woods.

The hairs on the back of my neck creep up. I take one step back from the window, then two, holding my breath. With a wave of my hand, all the shutters slam closed, and their bolts fall into place. The door shuts and locks. All of my candles go out aside from a single flame. I take two determined steps to the fire and kneel down before it.

Then I stare into the flames, concentrating. Gathering my power. Feeling the constant flow of the moon through the skies and of her light down to the land.

"Let them see me not," I say, then blow the fire out.

Love Spell

FOR THE GOOD of all and to the harm of none...

Dry one eggshell, and write the name of your intended on the shell in oil as it dries.

Next, crumble dried rose leaves in salt in a mortar and pestle, then add the eggshell once dried. Grind together with the intention in your incantation: *You love me in the light and in the dark. You love me for who I am not who you think I am. Love so pure and protected, love divine and never broken.*

Once the salt is pink in color you have ground it sufficiently. Sprinkle your salt on a morsel intended for your lover to eat. Any amount shall suffice. So mote it be.

Fucking hell. I have to tug harder to get my jeans unstuck from a thorny vine that snuck up on me. *All of this for a flower?* I grit my teeth and push through, shaking off the inconvenience and grateful I'm nearly done with the task.

I'm pleased to do a favor for a friend. That much, at least, is true. But the pleasure I feel in doing this errand for my friend is not without its vice. Namely, that I was not honest when I accepted the work. There was much I didn't say. For example, I did not say *I would rather do anything but attend this wedding. I would much rather waste my training on gathering florals for the upcoming event.*

Gritting my teeth I scan the forest for more of the blooms.

That is exactly what I agreed to do, pick a rare flower in an uninhabited region—apart from a supposedly powerful witch who hates all others.

I'm here at the edge of a quiet woods near sunrise because the wedding of Prince Adom and Princess Charlotte could not go on without the florals—this specific bloom that the princess *required*.

I have sought the florals throughout the woods. Even at this hour, the moon is bright enough that I can continue until I've gathered everything that is necessary and then some.

There, at the edge of the path, is another one of the florals I'm meant to collect. Its large, delicate, scarlet petals are beautiful...but so is any other flower. I trudge along, ignoring the stinging of the cuts on my arms as they heal in no time. A perk of my wolfen blood. The rate of healing is also why I'm a fighter, and a damn good one. *A fighter picking flowers...*

A crack behind me stops me in my tracks. A branch snapping under the weight of some creature. Pausing, I hold my breath and listen. The forest is alive with sounds, but none of them indicate anything other than woodland creatures in the underbrush and leaves blowing in the branches. Woods in the very last hours of night, when most of the creatures sleep or are bedding down.

Nothing out of the ordinary.

When I'm sure once again that no one is near, I bend and cut the floral, then place it into my pack with the rest.

Flower-picking. That is what my life has come to. I would wager all the money I've ever earned that the worst danger in this stretch of forest is me. There is nothing in particular for me to fear. I would have caught the scent in the wind long ago.

Still, I don't let my guard down.

Even if I'm only gathering florals.

As I search for more, the wedding itself looms far larger in my mind than any of the dangers to be found near this place.

I dread the upcoming event. As a wolf shifter who will never have a fated mate, I'm more than disinterested in the gathering.

Long ago I was cursed. No wolf will ever be mated with me. Without a wolf to be my fated mate, there is no companionship in my future. I've lived a lonely life in that respect, but the curse was not without a benefit. Without love, I've become one of the most highly trained and deadly forces defending the Crown.

Perhaps it was the curse that instilled this hatred of weddings in me. Perhaps—along with that decree for the rest of my life—they planted a seed of disgust that grew until it was full-blown derision.

I *despise* the very thought of love. And what is a wedding but the very pinnacle of love? The love between the married couple, yes, and of all the guests who have come to witness their union, and of the land they will rule. It will be a day overflowing with love. *Flooded* with love. The scent of it will be so thick in the air that it could suffocate a man like me.

A *shifter* like me.

The wolf that dwells in me does not disappear when I am in the form of a man. My heightened senses are with me always. I will never see in the dark the way a human does or scent the air the way a human does. I will always see the subtle nuances in the shadows and smell everything around me in the detail necessary for a lethal hunter.

An aggravated sigh leaves me. Even I've grown tired of my reluctance to do my part and accept that this is a wedding I must attend. Once I've completed the task I was asked to do.

Scenting the forest around me, I search for more of the fragrant blooms. Damp earth and budding leaves and half-dried bark surround me. With the moon high and the day of mundane activity wearing on me, I prepare to rest, although I do not wish to. So searching for more is what I do, even with my eyes heavy.

I'm used to sleeping in my traveling pack and can do without a tent on warm nights, but I tossed and turned for hours last night, my eyes hardly closing, and now I'm racing toward the end of this task. By the time the sun is high in the sky, I'll be gone. Back through the portal and to the palace to complete my service.

I've already collected hundreds of stems for the wedding over the past few days, but I will not take the chance of sending too few. Forty more, perhaps, or fifty. The sack itself is of a special kind, lined with the ability to keep the flowers, or fruits, or what have you, fresh and protected. Supposedly the witch in this very land cast a spell on it a decade ago. As I gaze through the forest, vaguely interested in her whereabouts, my heart races. The whispers of her are more and more like fairy tales. I'm not sure what to believe. All I know is that I am to collect the flowers and leave her be if I were to stumble upon her.

What a life to live. Alone in a land all to oneself. Perhaps she is cursed as well.

I move along the path in the growing dawn, every muscle in my body on the edge of readiness. I've spent a lifetime honing my natural skills in fighting, and now they are part of me. I keep my limbs loose, yet prepared to respond on a moment's notice.

Although I am so obviously alone and the very idea of this task being given to me is comical.

If I thought at all about the florals I'm collecting, each one would remind me that I will never have such a ceremony. I will never have a mate, and I will never have that connection which is stronger and more elemental than love.

I don't think of such things at all as I use my athame to cut this stem, then that one, just below the first leaf. I don't leave a path of destruction behind me. Each flower will have ample time to grow back and bloom again. That, too, is important to this ritual. The florals cannot have been gathered carelessly, with their roots pulled from the dirt. Their flowerings must be the only part taken so that life still dwells in them. The princess was as specific as she was excited.

It is gentler work than I am used to, of course,

but I do it with a soldier's precision. The florals are fragile, in their way. It does not take much force to slice the blade of the athame through the thin stalks. The athame has a handsome silver hilt, warm from being held in my hand for so many hours. It was carved and blessed to be true in its aim and strike as it must. It does not take a strike to gather a floral. Only a soft press, and the first leaves and the flowering come away without a fight.

The poison I have carried with me every day since the curse flourishes the longer I stay in this forest. It burns hotter when there are no other voices to distract me and when every plant I touch reminds me of the wedding.

A growl escapes my throat as I bend to collect the next floral, but I shake off the feeling of resentment and continue, listening for anything that may be approaching.

This territory, called Athica, is a long one, stretching from east to west and touching the ocean. There is only one being who is known to dwell here —the one solitary witch.

In Abrakearth to the south, however, there are shadow walkers. To the north, there are shadow fae. There is very little to prevent either of those from crossing this territory. Except for the threat of the witch of course. But how powerful could she really be against so many others? I've found no sign that either shadow fae or shadow walkers have ventured here, at least in recent days. I stay alert nonetheless, growing more and more curious about the witch.

In the back of my mind, I wonder if she knows I'm here.

I follow the path to the edge of the forest and finally emerge into a large clearing. It stretches away from the trees far enough that it could be a field or a valley. I tip my face toward the sky and drink in the sight of the stars. The dark night is littered with beauty. I don't mind being in the woods, but I can breathe easier under the open sky.

Keeping close to the trees, I move around the outside of the field, following the shallow dips in the land until I find a space that is not so visible. It is only a few steps down, but that will do for opening the portal. I do not need secrecy, but the shape of the land will focus the energy into its curve, gathering it closer and making it easier to send the florals through.

I pause on the low rise and look across the field. Its colors are pale in the moonlight, but as the dawn comes closer, the colors deepen.

A new day is beginning. A huff leaves me.

Perhaps that is why the heaviness under my eyes begs me to sleep.

I feel a strange ache in my chest. This land is beautiful. I've spent these last days in peace as I gathered the flowers, and despite my feelings about the wedding, I'm grateful that the mission was easy. A soldier cannot hope for better. I did not risk life or limb, was not injured, and gathered all that the royal house asked of me and more.

The pang I feel has nothing to do with a sense of failure.

It is more a sense of…curiosity. A longing I've not hoped for or even acknowledged in so long. The quiet thoughts of my mind are my enemy.

Again, I think back to the witch of Athica, wondering where she resides, as I've searched this land thoroughly.

Dropping the bag to the ground and ready to form the portal, I find myself wishing I had more time. The irony and hypocrisy, not wanting to be alone with my thoughts and yet not wanting to return, is not lost on me. It is a torture of my own doing.

I would have liked to see the witch's home. I would have liked to see the witch herself. Some rumors say she lives in a cottage. Others say she lives in a fortress underground. Still others say her house is invisible, and the sight of it can kill a man.

There is a curiosity that tugs me to her. It's unsettling.

The sun peeks through the tree trunks, gracing my arm with the first rays of dawn. The tiny cuts have all gone. I think sarcastically, *alas I can tell the prince I was not harmed in the errand.* A huff of a laugh bristles up my chest and a smirk tilts my lips up.

A breeze gusts through my hair, and—I smell something on it.

My body stills and a seriousness takes over. The scent is sweet and has the tone of magic to it, but not any magic I have confronted before. It is heady and enticing, like it is calling me to hunt. To find it. To give in to my own curiosity and forget the florals. To find whoever it is that causes such a scent to be in the world and press my nose closer to know her better.

Her? What thoughts plague me?

I shake my head, turning my face away from the breeze. I do not often have flights of fancy like that. It is not the kind of thing for a seasoned soldier to get the better of him. I will not let it get the better of me. The light grows and I stay focused on my task, although the scent is like nothing I've felt before and yet it is so familiar.

The portal, I command myself. At least to send the flowers through.

Birds fly out of the trees by my side, their calls echoing across the fields. I step down into the dip in the land, readjust my pack, and set about opening the portal.

The first step is to place the stone anchor on the ground. The anchor itself is not very large so that it can be carried long distances if necessary. I place a charged crystal into the space carved for it in the anchor. Energy hums all around me. I speak the words in a low voice, "Now you open, now I enter," and the portal opens.

It is small, perhaps the size of a mirror, to start with, but that is large enough for my purposes. I have gathered the florals and put them into bundles that can be rolled up and tied off. With a length of rope, I secure them together and find that they will not fit.

The magic gets louder as I press the portal farther open. It should not take much. An inch or two. I slot the bundle into the portal, lean my entire weight against it, and push.

With a final heave, the florals pop into the portal

and disappear, the surface shimmering like water on the surface of a pond. My shoulder hits the rippling barrier, and I pull back.

I won't fit through the portal as small as it is, but sending the florals was more difficult than I anticipated. Something feels off and a nervousness I don't appreciate comes over me.

Taking a few steps back from the portal I rest one of my feet on the low rise surrounding the small valley. The field around me is even brighter now. The sunrise is making the colors vivid, and I feel that pang again. That longing to spend more time roaming these fields without the weight of the florals on my back. To seek out something no one else has ever found so that I can see it with my own eyes. *The witch.* Even my wolf stirs at the thought.

On my next breath, the scent returns. As if I've summoned it with thoughts of her. It's faint, like it is coming from far off or does not want to be found, and yet it is so distinct from the grasses and flowers and trees that I cannot help but notice it. I'll never forget it as long as I live. Even in this moment I know that. I take another deep breath in spite of myself, holding it in and closing my eyes, trying to know more about it, but it is only a scent on the wind. It fades in a matter of moments, or I become used to it. My wolf whines.

Everything in my body tells me to seek out more of that scent.

My knuckles turn white as I clench my fists at my sides, warring with myself. There is no reason other than my own desire to seek out the witch. Something tells me it would not be difficult to find the source. I'm strong enough and fast enough to do it. After so many days picking my way through the forests and fields, I crave a run and a hunt. I need to feel my heart pumping from a real challenge.

But there will be no such thing to find. I already know that.

What this scent promises—a *match*—is not something I will ever have. The scent does not belong to a wolf, and even if it did, I will never be mated to one. And yet these feelings stir, unwelcome but so dominant.

I move toward the portal without realizing that the pang in my chest has become something more than curiosity. It is disappointment. The mission has gone well. I've done what I came here to do. And though I may never see this land again, it will make no difference to the rest of my life. I'm as cursed as I was before I came, and as cursed as I will remain after I leave.

This is not the time to let a wild urge overwhelm me.

I take one last look at the land that spreads out around me, remembering my duty and the only purpose I have to live.

Maybe, in another life, I would have broken free of my responsibilities and gone in search of the witch. Maybe I would have found her. Maybe we would have spoken, and she—who chooses to live alone amid all this beauty—would have understood what I have never been able to explain to other soldiers or wolf shifters.

I wish all of that, and the land, a silent farewell. It has been generous to me these past days, and I won't forget it.

Then I close my eyes, shutting all of it out, and prepare myself for my departure. Only to find that the portal refuses to open.

As goosebumps spread down my arms, I remind myself, the howl of a wolf is nothing to be distressed about. I live alone, and that means the woodland animals have nothing to be distressed about, either. The deer are free to roam. The wolves are free to howl. It is an unsettling sound so close to the cottage, but only because it had come as a surprise. There is something different, something that causes the feelings of earlier to come back stronger.

My sleep should not be so restless. My heart should not be as wayward as it is.

I am as safe as a person can be in my cottage. I have cast protective spells many times over. The walls and doors are sturdy, and the shutters are strong enough to survive even the heaviest of storms. Magic roams in every corner of my home. I am so divinely protected, I know this, and yet...

Yet I wake several times in the night and lie there, listening for the sound of someone approaching. As if I know that is what is coming although it has never happened in the years I've been here.

As the hours drift away, there is no sound of steps that come. No one approaches. No one comes close to Athica, let alone my cottage. They did not come close when my coven was alive, either, out of respect or superstition or both.

I almost wish they were not superstitious. I almost wish they were not afraid.

But perhaps what they believe about me keeps me safe.

I fall into a night terror of what happened before so fast and hard that I did not know it until it was too late. After that, I lie awake, staring into the dark and trying to convince my heart to settle down.

I drift off into an uneasy sleep that does not last. Even my trick of closing my eyes and *pretending* to be asleep does nothing. I resent it when the world starts to wake up around me, with the first bird calls of the morning echoing across from the forest.

"Fine," I grumble finally. Even with my eyes

closed, I can tell the sky is lightening through the slim gaps in the curtains. That is the danger of knowing my home so well, I suppose. I'm so attuned to every change that I cannot ignore the stirring of the morning. Whether I'm ready or not, it is coming, and it is only making me feel worse to lie in bed and try to force sleep that will not come.

So I push off the covers and stretch, long and luxurious, then step out of the bed as if I planned to be up this early and I'm not annoyed about the poor sleep I barely got.

There is no rush—I'm not going anywhere—so I stir up the fire and brew a pot of tea. I throw open the curtains and watch what I can see of the sunrise, gradually soaking the fields in rich greens dotted with pinks and purples and yellows. Beautiful colors. They have brought me so much joy in the past. I try to take that same joy in them now, but I do not feel much of it. My mind wanders back to the invitation and disappointing the prince.

I had thought the tea would bring me calm, but it doesn't. I tap my foot on the floor and breathe deeply and stretch—all things that would usually relieve this restless feeling.

No matter how many times I attempt to ground myself, sipping my tea and looking pointedly at the beauty outside my window, the feelings do not disappear.

Whose spirit is this? I do not like to think of such things as hauntings. The spirits may come and go as they please. It might even be comforting if some of my sisters returned in a spirit form to visit me.

This does not feel like being visited by a loved one.

It feels like loneliness, and the loneliness only gets worse. The cottage, which has always been snug and clean and well cared for, feels oddly empty around me. I have felt like this at times over the years since I lost my coven, but I never felt quite so…small. The world outside has never felt so huge, seeming to stretch away from me forever.

Anything could be out there.

That has always been true, hasn't it? It dawns on me as if so obvious, the unsettling feeling is longing. A part of my soul longs for more.

And if I wished—truly wished— I could be out there, too, farther than I've ever gone before. In a land where no one has ever heard of my coven. In a brand-new life that pretends it is whole and never lost anyone.

It's only a human thing to believe that there is something better on the other side of the forest or just beyond the next hill. That we could run far enough to leave behind the pain of our pasts. Maybe, after so much time alone, I'm willing to believe that any other life would be better.

"Not true," I whisper to the flowers, with the hot cup of tea in both hands and the warmth of its steam tickling my nose. "Not true. Look at you."

I go about my morning routine, washing my face and brushing my long thick brunette hair, all the while enchanting the day with unexpected blessings as I do each morning. I weave my locks in a simple braid and finally, I chose a dark blue cotton sundress with a pleated skirt and thin straps. Blue, the color for calming in magic.

Eventually, I tie on my pocket purse and throw open the door, half-expecting to find someone on the other side.

There is no one there. Only the slight chill of the night battling the morning sun.

With feigned ease, I stride across the yard to my stone oven, casting a quick glance over the well and the bench. They are the same as they were yesterday aside from a glistening layer of this morning's dew. My garden is damp, too, the soil soaking in the moisture before it can be burned away by the sun.

I do not know why I feel so lonely all of a sudden.

Worse than lonely—*alone*. I skim my fingers over the soil and find a seed, then grow a hasty cucumber and another potato. I cannot jump to my feet fast enough after I pull them out of the ground.

A feeling at the back of my neck brings goosebumps down my spine. Breathlessly, I turn.

There is nothing. The fields are empty. The forest —as far as I can see—is empty.

Goosebumps prickle on my arms and the back of my neck. I square my shoulders and make a point of looking all around, letting my eyes linger on every piece of the land.

"See?" I say under my breath. "There's nothing here. You did not sleep well, and that is all this is. The invitation is only an invitation."

There is no answer, of course. Except for my beating heart proving that it does not believe my excuse.

I don't run back to the cottage. I walk back with my head held high, pretending I do not feel so uneasy. Pretending I am safe here, and that I do not mind the lifetime that stretches out before me without anyone to pass the time with except the villagers who write to me for spells. That is enough for one person. It will be enough for me.

It is time to answer the invitation.

But first—

I scrub the cucumber and potato and chop the cucumber into slices to have with tea later. I find a place for the sweet potato in the kitchen. I breathe slowly and deeply, easing myself into the next task. I make a point to feel the calm of my home and the security of it all around me. The security that I have built.

When I've thought it over long enough, I find a glass pen and ink, then sit at my table and consider what to write.

There is no need to include many details. Prince Adom and Princess Charlotte will likely not read my reply, since there are people who do those kinds of things for the royal household. I bite my lip as I dip the tip of the pen in black ink, still feeling odd and lonely and somehow exposed, even though I'm safe in my cottage.

This reply is about *thanking* them for the invitation, first and foremost, so that's how I start. I tell Prince Adom and Princess Charlotte how grateful I am to have received it, and though I must decline, I wish them all the happiness in the world.

Then I sign my name at the bottom and spend a minute or two looking at my signature.

Is it…enough? Pretty enough? Elegant enough? Respectful enough?

They know I am a solitary witch without a coven, who lives in Athica and has not been seen by most people in years. And whoever opens this letter and marks off my name on the invitee list won't be paying attention to my signature, so I fold it up and seal it with a bit of wax and a pressed flower I made last summer.

Somehow, the sight of that flower, pressed into the purple wax, makes the uncertain feeling even more intense. As if this is a mistake. I don't often ignore my intuition, but venturing so far alone is simply not wise, no matter how curious I may be.

Without wanting to send off this message with loneliness clinging to the paper, with the snap of a finger I light a white chime candle in a brass candle holder. I concentrate on a spell to make sure there is no harm done—not even an uneasy feeling—in my denial.

"For the good of all and to the harm of none, my rejection will be met with understanding. My attendance is not required," I say aloud, testing the words. "Their love remains admired. With all that's meant to be, I'll stay here with fate to see."

I repeat the words again, using a fingertip to

trace the invitation script into the candle. On the third repetition, the spell takes hold and flows through the candle and out through the flame.

The candle flame dances in the softness of my exhale, and as my spell covers the paper and the words I have written, contentedness smooths out the harsher edges of my loneliness and doubt. I may have lost my coven. I may spend my days in a silence most people will hopefully never know. But the candle is proof—I am never truly alone. Not as long as I have my magic.

With that spirit and energized by the sight of the candle burning happily away, I get up and start gathering items for a gift to send as well.

"Ah yes!" I state as the perfect gift becomes so obvious.

That will be the perfect thing to send along with my message. A heartfelt thanks for the invitation, my regrets that I cannot attend, and a lovers' grimoire cast with a beautiful intention of a royal union.

This is the kind of project my sisters would have rejoiced in. Everyone would have had a part to play. There would have been playful arguments over what to include and who should cast the spells and which of us should be the one to carry it to the wedding.

I think of my sisters and their joy and wrap that

around me like a blanket and hum one of the songs we used to sing under my breath as I work.

Joy is going into this gift, not sorrow. Not the anticipation of grief. The anticipation of together-ness. Of happiness.

I find a small, beautiful wicker basket and empty out the fresh flowers I gathered earlier this week, although the lovely scarlet bloom lingers in my gaze as if it wants to be included. Then, in a small but lovingly made book I sewed myself, I write out several spells for a beautiful life together. Blessings on the ceremony itself. Blessings on the couple's new, combined life. Blessings on the first year of their marriage. Still more blessings on the many decades they will spend together.

Blessings for a long and fruitful life for *both* of them. I write out these spells with as much determi-nation in my heart as I can muster. It flows so easily and so lovingly. I hope Prince Adom and Princess Charlotte will have each other until the end of their days. I wish for them to have everything that I will not. My pen stills at the thought. Perhaps it is best I end my intentions here.

I gently place this little book of magic into the basket, but it looks too lonely there for what it is. The book needs a bit of company for the journey to the ceremony. More company than my letter alone.

More small miracles are the answer. Prince Adom and Princess Charlotte are royals. They have everything money could buy, but these smaller delights cannot be bought. They must be found and kept and given.

My heart lifts as I move around the cottage. I have saved many such small bits of magic over my years, and there was never an occasion like this to use them. As I open drawers that expand far beyond their physical limits, the spells allow more space than one could imagine so I may store all my trinkets neatly, I choose gifts that serve a specific purpose. I can only hope their warmth is still felt in the glass vial of phoenix fire and the vial filled with petals from divine roses that are no longer. Even holding these glasses bestows power and blessings, and for a few moments, I hold them in my palms, knowing the power and the gratitude that exists within the vials.

"Take that feeling with you," I whisper to the vials, then lower them to the basket. A wicker basket woven by a witch, flowers, and a hand sewn grimoire with blessings along with vials of the past that no one else could possibly possess. Surely, this gift will be met with awe and understanding that I wish them all the love in the world.

Just as the vials are about to drop from my fingers, a new sensation comes over me. Colder than before. Sterner than I felt in the last days.

The hairs on the back of my neck rise, just like they did when I heard the howl of the wolf. This time, it is no mere nervousness. The feeling is much more alarming.

Something's wrong.

A gasp leaves me as the vial drops from my hand. I feel it before it happens. The next moment, the wind bursts through my window. The panes of glass swing in on the hinges, banging against the opposite wall, and a gust of wind shoots across the cottage like an arrow, blowing out the candle before the wax is finished melting. I find my body tense, my hands shaking.

A crack of lightning sizzles through the air, scaring the breath out of me, and then the window goes dark. Rain pours down from the sky and beats on the roof. It is so loud, and so sudden, that I can't hear my own heartbeat, though I can feel it banging in my chest.

Something's gone horribly wrong.

I go to the window, blinking against the harsh

wind and hoping the glass doesn't break. I don't dare cast a spell at it in case the power is amplified by the lightning. I find the edge of the window and press it shut, even as more raindrops fly into the cottage, catching in my hair and wetting my face.

I just manage to shut it before more rain comes down harsher. These droplets are much sharper, like hail, but that is not what worries me most. Punishing. A cleansing but punishing rain.

What has happened? I fear the worst: I've angered the magic.

What worries me most is that the sky is not only darkened from storm clouds. It's dark as night outside. My eyes don't want to believe what I'm seeing, but they must—there's naught to see outside my window.

This must be something to do with magic, and powerful magic at that. There can be no other answer.

But there is no one in this land who is more powerful than I am.

There is not supposed to be anyone more powerful than I am.

The sky gets even darker, and a huge bolt of lightning flashes down from the sky, landing in the field with sparks that turn to flames and die away under the rain. That is what finally makes me act. I step back from the window and wave my hand. All the shutters close again. I send some extra power across them to make sure they are shut *tight* and bolted, then go hunting for a cloth to dry my face. Quite a bit of rain came through the open window.

I stand before the fire, letting it dry the damp places on my dress, and press my face into a cloth made by Elsma, who was the best seamstress in the coven before she died. If she were still alive, and still here, we would all be gathered at the fire right now, leaning close to speak into each other's ears and trying to decide what the storm meant and who had made it happen and what could be done about it.

I try to breathe through the realization that I must do this alone. This isn't even the time I miss them most. I miss my coven most on the longest days of summer, when the light seems like it will never end, and we could cast spells and sing songs and make each other laugh until we fell asleep under the open sky.

When the magic was playful, not like this.

Thunder booms and more lightning cracks down, and I can't think of anything but the rain that must be soaking the ground and turning the dirt to mud. I can't think of anything but the magic that is behind such a storm. *Where did it come from? Who did this? Who would have reason to do this? Did I make a mistake?*

I am the only one here. If they are hoping to scare me away or send me running to somewhere else...

That will not work. I have nowhere else to go.

Another thought occurs to me. Perhaps there is no one behind this, and it is only wild magic, and it may grow until it consumes all the land around me.

Or it may taper off, disappearing as quickly as it came.

I have no idea.

I look up at the ceiling while the rain comes down on me and pray to the moon for a sign.

Protection Spell

FOR THE GOOD of all and to the harm of none...

Burn sage, and with the ashes, mix into salt until black in color. Add to a mortar along with rosemary to focus your spell and chili flakes for a defensive measure. As you grind the ingredients state: *I am divinely protected, divinely guided, and am untouchable.*

Coat the black candle with olive oil and then sprinkle the black salt concoction to layer on the candle.

Light the candle with an obsidian stone near so the light may shine on it. As many stones as you wish to enchant. Allow the candle to burn to completion and then keep your obsidian stone by a draft in your home or by a window close to the front or back door. You may also keep the stone on your person for protective measures.

So mote it be.

What in the fuck just happened? This is not a pitter patter, this is a battering. Confused and frustrated, rain falls around me as I try again and again. The heavy water drops pound in a punishing way. I need to get the hell out of here… but it's not working. It's as if the portal is broken; the magic no longer allows the portal to open.

I grit my teeth and summon more power.

The portal is *about* to give—I can feel that it's seconds away from snapping open—when the sky opens up with thunder and lightning. My heart pounds and every hair stands on edge. Something's not right. A chill runs down my spine.

Thunder crashes and lightning sparks through

the sky not far away. Buckets come down on the top of my head. Wind gusts into my back and into my hands, swirling all around me and whipping my hair into my forehead, and darkness rolls overhead. I glance up without letting go of the portal and see nothing but black thunderclouds.

Fuck. The change is sudden and a different kind of anxiousness wraps itself around me.

Magic hits me along with the wind. That magic, whoever it belongs to, has to be causing the storm—it's too sudden and strong to be anything natural. Goosebumps race down my arms at the thought of the witch.

The portal thrashes in my hands, starting to snap shut, squeezing the hell out of my fingers in the process. I throw myself against it, bracing my feet hard on the ground and shoving with all my strength.

"Open," I order through clenched teeth. "Open, damn you!"

But the portal doesn't open. My only way of getting home closes before my very eyes as the rain crashes down around me. The crush around my fingers is stronger than a pair of boulders. It's not the worst pain I've ever experienced in the army. I'll bear it if it gets the damn portal to stop closing and let me through, but it doesn't stop.

Instincts take over to save my fingers and I yank my hands away as the portal chomps shut and dies, leaving nothing but a shimmer in the air.

My breath leaves me as I stare ahead as what just happened is not possible.

The curses I let out are drowned out by the rain. Thunder and lightning race across the sky in deafening bursts. Everything about this is wrong. I should have had enough power to get back. I don't know what magic could've shut it down like that.

I find the anchor on the ground and stand over it, every sense I have screaming a warning. Storms like this don't just come out of nowhere. This has to be related to the magic of this place. I haven't done anything to upset it. Not that I know of. I was warned to go unnoticed, and I thought I had.

I attempt to open the portal again, then again, until most of my crystals are entirely drained. Nothing happens in return for this effort except some minor crackles and fizzles in the air. I don't get the portal to reappear. Any hope of the portal working is drained as well.

I try one more time, rain drizzling down my back, then scoop up the anchor and shove it into my pack, fixing a glare on the space where the portal was only a minute or two ago.

The very portal that accepted all those florals, then shut me out.

A prickling in the back of my mind says that this is happening because of those thoughts. The ones of the witch.

With a final curse, I move into the forest. Dead set on finding her. Confronting her. And if this was not her doing, pleading for her aid in getting home.

It dawns on me as I walk: I am alone, surrounded by potential enemies north and south of here, with no shelter, no means of escape. *Fuck!* I cannot see more than a few feet in front of me. It is completely transformed from how it was only a short time ago. The darkness is thick under the trees, and I make my way under the cover of the branches using the flashes of lightning that manage to get through.

No matter how the storm began, I don't like it. I don't trust it. I want nothing to fucking do with whatever the hell just happened.

A short distance into the forest, I find a small clearing that is mostly sheltered by branches and stop at the bank of a gnarled tree trunk. I swing my pack—now sodden and twice as heavy as it was— down to the roots and dig out a few smaller crystals, these still pulsing with power. It is concentrated power, as these crystals are meant for communication over long distances, and they are among the more precious items in my pack.

These crystals are only to be used when there are no other options.

I am still searching for another option even as I place three of the crystals in a triangle in the vee of the largest tree roots and roll a fourth in the palm of my hand. Rain batters the branches above me. Plenty of the droplets seep through and land on my head. Some of them drop down the side of my neck and onto my clothes. Goosebumps prickle down my shoulders.

I don't see another option though. This is the last thing I wanted to do.

There's also no telling how long this storm will last or what level of damage it will cause before it passes. If I wait until then to attempt to make contact, I do not know how long I will have been missing, or what consequences might be levied against me.

My jaw aches with how hard I grimace at that thought.

I center my focus on the crystal in my hand and mutter the call. Resentment grasps my throat.

For a moment, I'm certain it will not work—that somehow even these crystals, hidden safe in my pack, were also drained in my attempt to widen the portal.

But heat flares in my hand, and there is a subtle vibration, and the spell takes, connecting across the lands to its match. It's fortunate that a connected crystal glows, otherwise I might not be visible to Jorge, the commander who swims into view on one of the crystal's facets. He's a human commander in the army and someone I greatly respect.

"Jorge," I say as Jorge's image shakes in the crystal. Somehow as concern mars his face, the rain comes down even harder, which I did not think was possible. The sound of it is contained in the clearing, so it seems even louder than it might if I was out in the brunt of the storm. "Can you hear me?"

His image wavers again, as if the distance between the crystals is too great to overcome. I grip it as tightly as I can without dropping it. Jorge's voice crackles, reaching me in fragments I can't quite make out.

Fucking hell.

"Can you hear me?" I ask again. "Jorge? Am I coming through?"

"—you returned?" he questions. "Ryker. I see you. Where are you? Have you made it back?"

"No." A peal of thunder crashes overhead as if the center of the storm is following me. "I sent the florals through, but when I went—" A crack of thunder interrupts me. The lightning is so bright and close that it illuminates the dark clearing for a few seconds at a time. There is so much of it that it cannot be caused by natural means unless the storm is swirling in a tight circle directly above where I stand. "When I tried to enlarge the portal, it...fought back."

"You've encountered hostile troops?" His voice is muddled but I shake my head in case mine is on his end as well.

"No," I state perhaps a little too loud. I wait through another burst of thunder. "The portal slammed shut and wouldn't open again—" A gout of water comes through the branches directly onto my shoulder and my lips form a tight line as I breathe once then twice through gritted teeth. "This storm came. I can't summon the portal. My crystals are drained."

Jorge nods. I shield the crystal with my hand so I can keep him in view. The droplets are drawn to the light like a magnet, and his image is magnified in grotesque ways when the droplets slide down the facet.

"Find the—"

This time, it's Jorge who is foiled by the thunder. His image turns cloudy, almost fading out, and I press myself closer to the tree, hoping to maintain our connection for a few more minutes.

"I couldn't hear you."

"Find the witch," he says, his expression calm, not betraying a hint of uncertainty about this order. "The witch. She is the only being there who has the means to help you and get you back if the portal isn't opening."

Something inside me shifts at the very thought of her. This woman whose reputation is vast and yet no one knows of her personally. Like a myth.

"She is the only one there," Jorge replies. "Find her. She can help you."

"Do you have any information on where she lives?"

Jorge opens his mouth, but before his words reach me, his image breaks apart in the crystal's facet and dissolves into shadows.

"Jorge," I call again with dull irritation as I heave in a breath that raises my shoulders and then I crack my neck.

He doesn't answer. The remaining power in the crystal flickers out, and the glowing light disappears just as Jorge's image did.

My jaw clenches as rain drips from my hair down my face and the sky lights up with more lightning strikes.

I lean my forehead against the trunk of the tree and bite back more frustrated curses. Jorge may not have known where the witch is rumored to live, but he might have had *some* information, which would have made my next task easier.

I give myself a few seconds, then pull myself up. I didn't become a soldier because such tasks are easy. I became a soldier because my greatest talents are fighting and using brute strength to force myself along any given path.

As the storm howls above me, I gather the crystals, then shoulder my pack and set out.

One step carefully after the other. Trudging through the mud, my senses are on high alert although my wolf is calm. Eerily calm. That grants me reprieve from worrisome thoughts.

Once I've reached the grassy field, it's slow going. The storm, which seems to be gathering impossible strength, turns the soil under my feet to sludge. Wet grasses cling to my boots. The light of the moons is almost nonexistent behind the black clouds, and the lightning strikes do not let me see more than a few feet ahead.

I wait through enough lightning flashes to get some idea of where I am. This is the same side of the forest I came out of when I finished gathering the florals, and there was no sign of anyone living on the paths in this direction. I didn't see anything to suggest a dwelling on my way to open the portal.

The witch must be living somewhere else.

A heady combination of doubt and curiosity crash inside me like a storm. It's not only my curiosity that guides me now. It is my *duty* to find the witch. It is my *duty* to ask her for assistance in recharging my crystals.

Once again, the world—or the gods—seem to be aligning with my private desires, which rattles me. I couldn't have imagined a circumstance that would send me through a violent thunderstorm to satisfy my curiosity about a witch no one has seen in years.

But I did everything I could to open that portal. If it is fate that slammed it shut, then I cannot argue against that. Not in any way that sends me home without searching for the witch.

My wolf stirs at the thought, and it urges me forward.

I travel during the flashes of lightning, squinting through the heavy rain to catch a glimpse of the forest on the other side of the fields. If I cannot find her dwelling here, I may have to begin searching the trees, which will be far more difficult.

But I live for the challenge. For intrigue to be satisfied.

With a slight grin at the thought of finding her and having a story to tell, I carry on. Hours pass in the early morning and I don't stop. I refuse to give in until I've found her. The mud sucks my boots down into it, and my thighs begin to burn from pulling them back out again. The rain is cold on my skin, but my muscles warm from the work of moving me and my gear across the field. It is a comforting sensation. My body is used to taxing physical work, and when I am set to a task like this, my mind calms and sharpens.

The field seems endless in the dark and the rain, as if I'll be walking across it forever, trapped in a vortex of magic that is meant to imprison me here.

I have the feeling time is passing. The *day* is passing. Sometimes I think it is passing too quickly, but then it feels like I have been trudging through the mud forever.

The line of trees on the opposite side of the field

begins to materialize in the distance. I keep my eyes focused on the sharp shapes of the trees whenever the lightning illuminates them. I don't think of the possibility that the witch will be tucked away in some far-off place that I cannot find. She will be here somewhere, even if it takes me days.

I simply keep moving.

Another shape begins to appear in the lightning flashes. It's a gap in the trees—or rather a shape in *front* of the trees. I angle myself toward it and press on until… My breathing slows and a warmth runs through me. Stillness settles and finally. Fucking finally.

Yes, there is something here.

A garden plot, I think as a smirk forms on my face, turned to mud, and a smaller structure—an outdoor oven, maybe. It is hard to tell in the rain.

And then there is the cottage. Its pointed roof is the shape I saw from a short distance away.

I have to pause to catch my breath. It must be her. *The witch.*

My body's warmed up and used to traveling with the weight of my pack pushing me down and the mud slowing me, so when I stop, my heart keeps running. Thundering itself as the lightning crashes around me.

Now that I am here, within sight of a dwelling—and it must be the witch's dwelling, as there is no one else in this part of the land—the rumors I have heard flood my mind.

The witch of Athica is said to be a recluse who lives alone and despises all other beings.

She's also said to be all-powerful, which some say is the reason she lives alone—that her powers are too dangerous to exist side by side with others.

I'm steps away from finding out if these rumors are true. If they are, I may be steps away from my own death.

I shake out my shoulders and head for the house. More eager than I've ever been, my wolf pushes me forward, ever restless and on the prowl.

All I could find in the grimoire was that a storm of this magnitude comes when a soul attempts to evade fate. The knowledge clings to me and yet I cannot make sense of it. Surely, there must be something else. Or someone else who has brought this on.

Secure in my cottage, I close my eyes and listen to the sound of the rain. It's a meditation of sorts. It calms my frayed nerves and gives me a sense of control. At first, I try to pick out individual drops on the roof, then think about the pattern of the down-pour, then concentrate instead on the inside of the cottage. I whisper for it to tell me its secrets. I'm only met with the pounding of the rain and its anger. So I wait, listening and waiting and contemplating if

I may have missed something. There must be something…or someone that I have yet to discover.

My cottage is clean and warm and snug. I'm safe inside, and even safer because of the storm.

I am safe.

I breathe in deeply and out even slower, concentrating on the safety I've built instead of the loneliness of it. If my coven still existed, we'd be settled in for the storm by now. The rain is still much too loud for any real conversation, but there are other ways to communicate. We could have written notes, or sat next to each other and worked on spells, or sewed, or cooked. My elder sister would have harnessed the anger of the storm by collecting its water and at that thought, I nearly run for a jar to set it outside but I hesitate. Something inside of me screams not to open the door. My intuition makes me pause.

For a while, I lose myself in memories. I can't remember another storm as strong and sudden as this one, but it's not as if the weather was always sunny and mild. There was the snowstorm that kept us inside for a week straight, with bitter winds and drifts coming halfway up the door. There was the spring freeze that turned the air so cold it hurt to breathe. It was years and years ago. But I remember how I felt…at peace.

We'd *all* danced in a circle in the field, the wind in our hair, until the moons came up. Grateful for the change and the cycles.

Oh—I have so *many* happy memories. They all reassure the same: the storm will be over soon. In this world nothing lasts but everything moves on.

I tell myself that time passes slowly because I'm waiting for it to pass. I keep listening for the rain to let up.

The rain on the roof doesn't soften. It doesn't get quieter. I open my eyes and stare up at the ceiling. It's hard to see with so little light. The only real brightness comes from flashes of lightning. Black clouds at this time of the afternoon just can't last. It is past midday now, though I can't tell exactly how long it's been. With a snap, I light the candles along the windowsill, and ten or so tea lights brighten the space. The flames are small but dignified and useful.

I pass time with a meal of seasoned bread and soft cheeses and delicious jams, then I pay a lot of attention to the steps of brewing a fresh pot of tea. It's chamomile, to calm my nerves. The spoon stirs itself as I watch the ripple of the motion in the teacup. It really does not take long to fiddle with the blend and boil the water and watch it steep, but I drag out as many of the steps as I can, then sip a cup of tea as slowly as I would if it was part of a ritual.

The storm *still* does not let up. The irritation and unsettled feelings it brings are unwelcome.

My heart beats faster at the idea that it might never let up, and the field might slowly fill with water and cover the cottage.

That will not happen, I promise myself sternly. There is too much earth around me. It will absorb the rain, and more flowers will bloom if the sun comes out.

When the sun comes back out. And *when* the sun comes back out, I will take my reply to Prince Adom and Princess Charlotte to the letter box along with the gift, and soon all will be well.

I trace the path to the royal palace in my mind, wandering over the path through the woods, which I know very well; over roads I know less well; and finally through the city that surrounds the palace. I picture booths on the market streets where I once stopped to haggle over items with the rest of the coven. I picture pubs and inns and shops decorated for the royal wedding. I picture a bustling city with guests from all over the world gathering ahead of the ceremony and passing the time with dancing and games and conversation. People will be up at all hours of the night. There will always be someone talking. The excitement will grow until the day of the wedding, and then it will spill into the streets with nothing but joyous celebration.

In the stories they tell afterward, they will have been within arm's reach of Princess Charlotte's gown and close enough to hear the vows she and Prince Adom will speak to each other. Mothers and fathers will tell their children stories of the day for years, and children will fall asleep hoping that one day they'll be able to go to a royal wedding, too.

I get carried away with the vision of it and have to cough to clear my throat. Look at me—a few hours alone in a storm, safe in my cottage, and I'm having all kinds of feelings about a royal wedding that I do not want to attend.

Perhaps I should lie down and go to bed for the night. It must be toward evening. It is earlier than usual, that is true, but it is so dark that the time does not matter much.

If the storm isn't going to let up, then the sound could send me to sleep. It's not so different from the sea.

I have just committed to the idea when there is a knock at the door.

My body freezes, my legs as stiff as stone. I'm in a

half-crouch, stuck between sitting and standing, and my thoughts are filled with the rain. Surely, I did not hear a knock. Surely, it was the rain or the wind—some element of the storm. A piece of earth blown across the hills and slapped wetly on the door.

But that knock—that imagined knock, I only thought it was a knock—did not sound wet, like a piece of earth. My heart bucks and a fear I recognize all too well comes over me.

I do not move, other than my pounding heart. It was nothing. It was nothing, and I have nothing to fear.

Another knock comes.

This one is undeniable. Despite the rain, so loud on the roof that I can hardly hear my own breathing, and despite the wind, which howls past the cottage, that is unmistakably someone's fist pounding at the door. My throat dries and tightens. Did I not cast the spell to not be seen?

I imagine the size of the fist it would take to make that sound, audible over the rain, and the strength someone would need to possess. Even to reach the cottage in the first place cannot have been easy.

Dread fills me, chilling me from head to toe. I wave a hand at the shutters out of an old habit, but they are firmly shut and latched so tight that even my panicked magic does not budge them.

Whoever is outside cannot get in...unless they have the strength to break down the door or punch through my protection spells and the walls itself.

More questions flood my mind, carrying on the wave of my dread. Who would come here in the middle of a terrible storm? Who in all the lands would think to knock on *my* door? I know the rumors that are said about me in every village I have ever visited, because I have had a hand in starting those rumors. On the few occasions that I've left the cottage and spent time in cities and villages since I lost my coven, I have made a point of asking a quiet question or two to someone in a tavern who looks like they are fond of travel.

I do not exaggerate much. I am true to the extent of my powers, which are considerable in comparison to someone who cannot wield magic. I am also true to my desire to be left alone.

I have heard there is a witch in Athica who lives by herself, I will say, keeping my voice low and checking over my shoulder as if I expect to be over-heard. *I have heard she is powerful and angry. Have you heard of this witch? She requires many miles of space around her cottage or else...* I let the person I am talking to fill in the blank of what *or else* might mean.

Gossip is a tried and true way to put information into the world. Travelers need some form of payment for their presence at an inn, and a neat piece of gossip is a way to form quick bonds with other people. I know these travelers.

And yet someone is here. In all the years no one has dared. Perhaps they know not where they are or who I am. A lost wanderer in the storm. Empathy overwhelms me but still I am wise to keep my guard up.

Cautiously, I finish standing up, shaking myself out of my frozen, indecisive state.

It is only a few steps to the kitchen, where the athame hangs from a hook, cradled in a leather sheath. I swing the sheath over my head and pull it into place on my shoulder, then draw the athame.

I am more grounded the moment my fingers close around the silver hilt. The blade is sharp and well-maintained, and I have practiced with it for years.

A deep exhale steadies me as I wave a hand at the grate. A roaring fire springs up, filling the cottage with flickering orange light. The flames leap higher and higher, throwing heat out of the grate as well, and the power settles me even more.

There. Armed with a blade and with my powers, I face the door as a third knock forces the wooden door to tremble.

With a few deep breaths, I approach the door, leaving a foot or two of space between myself and the thick wood. On the other side is a stranger.

Still, I wait for a few more seconds, half of me praying that this strange visitor will disappear back into the rain and half of me praying that they will knock again. It is such an odd sensation that I feel almost dizzy with it. Or is that another shift in the magic? I cannot tell. A person at my door is *so* out of the ordinary that I can do nothing but face each second as it comes.

"Who goes there?" I call out. My voice does not waver. Strength finds me even still. I imagine my coven at my back, waiting with their chins held high, armed with their own powers and their faith in me.

That is always how they were. That is why they decided to go and fight in the war.

"I am alone," a voice says through the door, rumbling and gruff. Strong, even through solid wood. "And my portal has failed me. My commander"—a peal of thunder drowns out a few words—"come to you. He said you may be able to help." My first reaction is one of shock. I am stunned. There is a man outside my door. With a voice that brings a certain feeling to the depths of me that I haven't felt in so long.

I push aside the delicious sound of the being's voice and focus on his words.

"Your commander?" I question. What reason would a commander have for sending a soldier here? To *my* lands, where I am the only person for miles? What business would an army have? "Why are you here?" The thinly veiled anger is deliberate. "This is my property," I call out.

"I came to collect flowers for a wedding," he says, his voice seeming carefully tense. I wish I could hear him better, but I would have to open the door to do that, and I will *not* be reckless about opening the door. Instead I stare at the intricately carved doorknob. The metal holds a spell within it. *No one shall pass who wishes me harm.* I remind myself of that spell as I soak in the stranger's tale.

Flowers for a wedding? Who sends a soldier to collect flowers for a wedding?

"Show them to me," I tell him. "Bring them to the window." I'm lifting my hand to open a pair of the shutters when he makes a sound.

"I sent them through my portal before it failed. I don't have them any longer."

A sarcastic laugh leaves me. How utterly ridiculous a lie. "Then how can I trust you?"

There is another long pause. My heart flutters, and it is not the flutter that warns me of danger. It is the flutter of curiosity. Who is this man? And what has truly brought him?

I shake my head, trying to get rid of that feeling. Curiosity brings danger. It can make a person forget to protect themselves.

The curiosity I feel won't leave me alone. More questions come to mind. What if it was this soldier who changed the magic in the land? What if *he* was the one who summoned the storm? There's another shift around me and it's then I hear the crack of thunder far too close.

"I am at a loss—" He raises his voice and then pauses again to let another loud crash of thunder die down. "I do not wish to disturb you," the soldier says, starting again. "But with the rain and the lack of a portal, I am trapped." The smallest break in his voice speaks of his honesty. "And I am at your mercy."

I cannot speak.

I search for the words to reply, but I can't think of what to say.

"I ask," he continues, "that you take pity on me. I will not stay long. Only as long as it takes for my portal to charge. Then I will go and leave you in peace."

It is not the first time a being has been at my mercy. Many beings who cannot cast spells but need one to get by have been at my mercy. I have received letters from frantic mothers and desperate fathers. I have heard from determined daughters and sons who will not rest until they have a solution. I have received a great many requests for mercy in the words that pour off the pages in my letter box.

My heart aches with empathy as if I'm the one who's cut off from home. Yes, I have lived in the cottage alone for the years since my coven was taken. I kept our physical home, but not the people who *made* it home, and I have been homesick for them more often than I haven't.

I know what it is to be far from everything you know without a way to get back.

I wave my hand at the door, undoing the latch and the bolts, then pull it open fast, before I can lose my nerve. If he can step through the doorway, he may enter. It is as simple as that. I will aid him in leaving this place as soon as the storm passes.

Outside, it is very dark from the thunderclouds, but more lightning burns across the sky, and there he is.

Something shifts wildly when I open the door. My heart won't behave, and my lungs don't know what to do. The sight of him…it does something to me I've never felt before.

He is tall and broad and muscled, wearing leather armor. Every inch of him that I can see is soaked from the rain, and dark hair runs in streaks across his forehead. He does not look like the kind of man who would ever need someone's pity. Certainly not mine. He is too strong. His presence overwhelms me. The shadows from my fire cast shadows on his sharp features, and it is like a gust of wind has come into the house and stolen my breath all over again.

My curiosity is no less powerful. It feels like a fire raging through me.

This soldier is the most gorgeous man I have ever seen.

A Spell Jar for Courage

RECIPE REQUIREMENTS:

A jar with a cork lid to carry the spell

A pinch of salt to cleanse and purify

Tiger's eye crystal for courage

A sprinkle of cinnamon (or a stick of bark) for abundance

Orange candle to seal the jar

Add your ingredients one at a time, stating the intention and purpose of each ingredient as you touch it. As the wax seals the jar, state the following:

For the good of all and to the harm of none, I am my own hero. Within me I possess the courage to open every door. I am able to walk through any space I desire. I am guided, protected, and being shown all possibilities for my higher self with strength. There is nothing that can stop me for I am capable and worthy. Courage walks beside me and holds my hand when I am in need.

When the wax has covered the lid and sealed the spell in the jar, blow out the candle and whisper, "So mote it be." Keep the jar in a safe place and shake if necessary to remind yourself of this truth: you already possess all the courage you will ever need.

If I had seen this woman in battle, I'd have died right there without striking another blow. Her beauty is a gift from the gods. I've never seen a soul so lovely. From her dark hair with waves that caress her face as the wind slips between us, to her striking hazel eyes that spark mischief and wisdom. She embodies a power in her slender frame that is draped in such delicate cloth.

I don't think I could look away even if I wanted to. I'm entrapped and I do not fear it. My body wishes to bow to her. It is as overwhelming as it is soothing. Laying eyes on the witch is like coming home.

She's tall, though not nearly as tall as I am, and the curves under her dress are shapely, mouthwatering spells. Her eyes in the firelight are a color I can't name. I need to take her face in my hands and draw her closer so I can put a name to that hue, but my training keeps me in my place. My fingers itch to explore every inch of her skin. She's intoxicating and I have barely breathed her in.

My orders were not to find the witch and lay claim to her. My orders were to find her so that she might help me charge my crystal and find a way out of here. I have a duty to uphold the honor of my oath. And yet it all seems to shatter the moment I scent her mouthwatering fragrance. It's nearly terrifying, the pull I feel to her.

The problem is that my oath seems to be no match for the fullness of her lips and the red flush on her cheeks. Those things, together with the gorgeous body hidden under her dress, have caught the attention of my wolf.

It stirs inside me, demanding that I inhale deeper, demanding to get closer to her scent. It is the same scent I caught on the wind—the one that made me burn with curiosity.

Heat engulfs me in an instant, and it is far stronger than the urges that struck me when I thought I was mere minutes from returning home. It's as if the fire has jumped out of her grate and into my blood. I bite back a growl and plant my boots on the muddy ground, using all the power of my muscles to stand still.

This does not matter to my wolf. My senses sharpen, telling me more about the lines of her face and the pulse beating in the hollow of her throat and her quick, shallow breathing. The witch grips an athame in one hand, and her posture tells me she knows how to use it, but her pupils are blown large and dark with interest. The scent coming off her now is fresh and even more intoxicating. There is a pull between us—some recognition, I think, or that is what my wolf wishes it to be.

The witch cocks her head slightly to the side and inhales, shifting the air around her and sending more of her scent into my veins as I pray for control. As I demand it from my wolf. This was a mistake. This woman…she bewitches me. I am sure of it.

"You," she begins, adjusting her grip on the athame. "Are not human."

"No. I am a shifter." I barely get out. As if I am breathless before her.

"I see…your eyes…" She takes a small step forward. The witch—this beautiful creature—is close enough for me to reach out and touch, yet the space she leaves between us is intentional. I do not breach it. If I do, I will not stop until I have satisfied my wolf. Until I have satisfied myself.

She gazes into my eyes, her own bright. "They are sharp and gray. Your wolf wants..." The witch looks for another long moment, then takes a sharp breath. "Your wolf wishes to hunt."

With a step back, her hand raises, and the door seems to obey her. Her hand is on the wood by the time I put my hand up to stop it. The pressure of the door seems greater than it should be. Even if the witch pushed it hard, it should not be swinging so heavily into my hand.

Magic. The power of the witch.

I have more strength than the door, though I must adjust my stance and engage my arm to hold it. This door must not close on me. She must not send me back out into the rain. Not only because of the crystals, but because my wolf is nipping and growling and demanding to be near her, and he will howl for hours if he is denied.

"Please. I...I will not cause you harm." Not an ounce of shame is felt although my plea is desperate.

Her hand tightens on the door, rising an inch like she might try to slam it shut in my face, but after a few beats she lowers her hand and steps back once again although the door does not budge an itch. Still I fight against its push.

The witch's eyes lower, to the doorknob I grip.

"You may come in." Her voice low, testing something on the tip of her tongue. With her permission, the magic pushing the door subsides and although my heart still races, everything around me seems to slow. With one breath, I look at her and easily push the door open.

I step through the threshold and shiver at the sudden change in temperature. A fire burns in the fireplace, throwing heat and light into a good-sized main room. It is a cozy place with a blue velvet sofa and a colorful chair by the fire. A quilt lays in a basket between the two. There's a small table by the window with jars of herbs and crystals strewn about it. Farther into the cottage, I can make out the kitchen and another table with four chairs around it. Many shelves line the walls, and there are crystals, books, and spell jars everywhere. A journal lays open on the chair closest to me and as my eyes turn to it, the thing closes on its own. Sharply and with an authority that catches me off guard. There are enough odd curiosities to look at for days, but I only spare them a short glance. My wolf is hungry for the sight of the witch.

With a few steps backward, she puts a few feet between us, her brow creased, then waves her hand at me in an odd way. Her slender fingers each taking a turn in a quick wave. As if she reads me like she reads the books that lay everywhere in this place.

I had not known how much rain was weighing me down until it lifts off. I feel her magic on my skin, and a low growl works at the back of my throat. I swallow it down before I can let the sound loose. We have only just spoken for the first time. I do not wish to frighten her with the growls of my wolf.

The rumors promised the witch was all-powerful, but perhaps I didn't know what that meant. With a wave of her hand she casts a drying spell. Lifting away water from my clothes and bag and boots, leaving me warm and dry. The change is sudden and leaves me still questioning the magic she possesses. It seemed to take no effort at all.

"Thank you," I say instead, swallowing thickly, and surprised at how much control I've gained by simply being welcomed. At being under her spell.

"You're welcome," she answers softly, bowing her head just slightly which causes her hair to brush against her collar. My mouth waters at the sight of her bare skin exposed at her neck. My cock stirs and

I feel heady with thoughts I should not have. "Come over to the table, would you?"

I follow her to the table. No light—except for the lightning—shines onto the surface. On the edge of the room candlelight flickers but this space seems different. It is clearly a worktable, with a crystal ball in the center. There is a small stack of cut flowers, some lengths of ribbon, more jars and crystals, and a little wicker basket.

The witch pauses at the table, her eyes flickering over her things as if she expects something to be missing.

"What is it you used to summon your portal?"

I swing my backpack off my shoulder and let it rest on the floor, then reach inside for the anchor and the crystal I used before. I show her without speaking. I know not of what has happened to my voice as I obey this witch without question. Amusement and curiosity has taken over my decades of training.

"And do you hold them like you are now?"

"No."

I bend down and place the anchor on the floor, then place the crystal in its place as well.

The witch's eyebrow lifts, but she does not seem to be surprised—merely curious. I feel that way about her. The more I look at her, the more stunning she appears to me. Every feature I linger on becomes more elegant. More beautiful. More intriguing. I curl my fingers into my palms, keeping them still.

While she studies the anchor, I study the witch. Her hair curls wildly in the humidity of the storm. Her dress looks well-worn but also well-made.

She meets my eyes, and my wolf lets out a *yip* of pleasure. The witch blinks a few times, as if she could hear it, and moves closer to the table. She places one hand on the crystal ball, the tips of her nails clicking against the crystal as she does, and stretches the other out toward the anchor and my crystal as if to offer energy to it. To charge it with her own power.

There is a faint flicker in the air above the anchor, as if the portal is about to return, but it does not.

The witch frowns, then opens her hand wider. This time, the flicker is even lighter.

She makes a soft noise of irritation, then tries a third time.

Nothing. There is not so much as a shadow.

The witch rolls her shoulders and stretches her wrists. She does not reach for the crystal ball again. Instead, she extends both hands toward the anchor.

Her shoulders square and her body steadies as she faces the anchor. My gods, she's fucking gorgeous. I wish nothing more than to ravage her as she harnesses such power. It takes great effort to snap out of it.

I realize I'm holding my breath in anticipation and let it out as subtly as I can. Her magic, it seems, is the kind that can be offered through the air, and I find myself fascinated.

She has long, graceful fingers and a confident bearing about her, as if she recharges crystals every day before breakfast and does much more complicated spells every night before bed. This is a woman who *knows* her power.

The surge is strong, but no portal appears. Nothing happens. No shadows. No flickers. It did not work.

The witch drops her hands to her sides, saying something sharp under her breath, and closes her eyes tightly. Fucking adorable. Her little hiss of dissatisfaction. My cock twitches and for a moment, I forget all reason.

I wonder what her thumb would feel like under the pad of my thumb. I wonder what her mouth would taste like.

This feeling—this curiosity and desire—is not to

be trusted. Yes, my wolf wants to know everything about her, wants to *claim* her, but I am alone in a land without a portal. The witch is supposed to be all-powerful. Why is she unable to charge the crystal? Why can't she send me home? The questions tick and I remind myself not to trust her. Not to trust a damn thing about any of this. I shouldn't be having these feelings—never. I'm meant to be alone.

The witch opens her eyes and holds her hands out to the anchor. More power moves through the air between us, and once again I find myself holding my breath. The air is magnetized and the pull is undeniable. Her magic floods the room with an intensity that nearly pushes me over.

But nothing happens to the portal.

"I do not know why your crystal is not charging —why I cannot charge it." She frowns at my anchor, chewing at the inside of her lip. She looks to the shuttered windows. "Perhaps it's the storm," she whispers as if to herself.

The rain beats down harder on the roof as if the storm heard her. Three peals of thunder come, one after the other, and lightning sizzles near the cottage. It sounds like it might have touched down in the field. All the hairs on the backs of my arms stand up.

I do not relish the idea of going back out into that storm. It should be waning by now, but instead it's getting stronger. If I were to go outside, I would have to huddle close to the cottage. With lightning like that, it is too dangerous to cross into the forest. My gaze shifts to the witch…and then I wouldn't be here with her. And all this curiosity.

"May I stay here tonight?"

Our eyes lock. Her beautiful gaze is wide for a few beats of my heart. She's completely still as if the very notion I'd stay here rather than in the depths of the storm hadn't occurred to her. Has she never had another visitor before? Is she…*confined* in this cottage by the powers that be? Is it so strange to seek the only shelter in a violent storm?

She blinks, her eyelashes fluttering, and I feel like I've been put under a spell. I do not trust the intense need my wolf has for her or the interest I have in her. I do not trust the way her magic failed to charge my crystal.

I do not trust *any* of what has come over me, starting with the desire to leave my responsibilities behind and explore until I found the source of that scent. I do not trust the hold the beauty of this land had on me. I do not trust the storm that seemed to conspire to keep me here.

Every instinct I have from the army warns me that this cottage—and a night spent with this enthralling witch—may not be any less dangerous than the violent storm raging outside. It warns that I might be better off taking my chances with the lightning.

"I..." The witch's hand comes up to the collar of her dress, and then she drops it back to her side. There is more color in her cheeks now. Is that because of the power she used or because she is looking at me? Is it because she is too warm in her dress with the roaring fire in the grate? "I only have one bed," she finishes.

My cock stirs again, and I can hardly contain my desire as her lips part just slightly. This woman could be the death of me, and I would gladly welcome it.

She spoke so quietly that I could almost pretend I did not hear. I could ask her to repeat herself, if I was willing to pretend. But my eyes were locked on her lips from the moment she started speaking, so I saw her mouth form the word *bed*.

I crave to take her to bed.

One bed. There is nothing my wolf wants more than to take her to bed.

He scented her and hasn't stopped pushing for

more. He can smell every part of her, and the sweet, floral scent is driving him wild. *Hours* would not matter to him at all. When my wolf is in full control, human concepts like time do not mean anything, and that part of me is becoming more needy with every second I stand here.

My muscles tense and relax, straining against my wolf. She is a witch and this is not real. It is the only logical conclusion.

I don't let the desire drive me wild. I'm a soldier. Trained and hardened.

I can withstand a wild desire from my wolf. I can keep him under control.

I can keep myself under control. My hands flex at my side as I glance back at the door, the rain pounding against it.

The storm or the siren in front of me. Fucking hell. My eyes drift back to the gorgeous woman, and I hate the reality that I will never mate. There is no wolf in the world for me. I am fated to be alone, which means these desires can only hurt me.

Because *if* I tasted her—if I touched her—if I attempted the ritual to claim her as mine—

It would fail. I cannot claim her as mine. I will not have a mate. No wolf will ever be my fated mate.

But, a small voice in the back of my head says, *she is not a wolf.*

Those thoughts are so far down any potential path that I should not even be having them, yet I cannot stop the images from filling my mind. I have only heard a handful of words out of her mouth, and I can already imagine how her moans would sound. I have not touched her, but I can imagine how her sweet curves would feel under my palms.

I swallow down all the feral noises I want to make and the filthy words I want to say. I forcefully stop thinking of all the delicious images of her spread out on a bed or in a pile of blankets on the floor. I do not let a single image come to my mind except for what is right in front of me—the witch, standing near her worktable, watching me right back. She swallows thickly and my eyes are drawn to the little dip in her throat. *Fuck me.*

I cannot take my eyes off her. I cannot pretend I want to look anywhere else. I cannot pretend I would rather be out in the storm, smelling mud and wet grass and lightning.

"I just," she starts, a flush creeping up her cheeks. "There's only the one bed."

I nod my head without thinking, hoping it looks polite and restrained. "I can sleep on the floor."

$\mathcal{I}$'m out of the habit of existing in close quarters with others. It's been far too long and I find myself out of sorts. Almost curious but also apprehensive with every sound he makes.

I should've realized that before, I suppose, but no one has stepped inside my home since I lost my coven. That also means no one has slept under my roof since then. No one has needed anything of me since then. The shifter's presence is as if the storm is now brewing inside me.

It's not that he is loud—he is not. He is almost entirely silent. Which I find intriguing. He's quite large with broad shoulders and his handsome form is at odds with the cozy warmth of my home.

By the time I offer him a bed on the floor, it *has*

to be late evening. The bed consists of an array of pillows and a knitted chenille comforter on top of three thick quilts, one of which I've had since I was a little girl. It's enchanted and the fact that he held it without consequence is a good sign. I remind myself of that as I shift under his heated gaze. The sound of the rain has carried me—both of us—through the day. The hours came and went. It is still, I think, earlier than I would normally go to bed but—

I do not know how to converse with the wolf and my thoughts are preoccupied by the absence of magic. What exactly has happened? Nerves prickle their way through me and leave me with unease. So he should sleep, so I may think of a way to undo all of this. Immediately.

I do not think I could fall asleep now even if I did get into bed. The idea of drifting off to the sound of rain is laughable with this muscled wolf taking up all the room in the cottage. It seems so commonplace to offer him tea and food, but he insists he does not need either. Still he looks at me, nearly through me, as if he is starved. It's unsettling in a way I've not felt. The heat and tension are palpable although I pretend they are as nonexistent as his appetite.

I've been alone so long that even a single, tall, handsome soldier is enough to take my breath away.

Swallowing thickly, I ask him if he needs anything, to which he shakes his head no. It's odd how I long for him to tell me "no" so I may hear the rough timbre of his voice and even odder that the moment I have that thought, he does so.

"No, thank you," he says, and my heart betrays me with a little flip and then a skip in my chest. I find it hard to breathe every time I look at him. I cannot just go about my bedtime habits while he stands there.

I have so many questions for him that my mind buzzes like a beehive, but the tension keeps them trapped inside. It is so thick between us that my face will not cool down. I must be as red as the midsummer roses along the back gate. My heart beats hard, as if he's watching and waiting for me undress. I'm only standing at my worktable, but I feel exposed—and desperate to get behind his leather armor to the soul concealed inside.

I keep asking myself what it is about him that makes me feel this way, but surely it's obvious, I've not seen a man in so long. Let alone one so…delicious. Hardened muscles and rough stubble… I am a woman after all…and not blind to his charm.

I pat my hands on the skirt of my dress and steady myself.

"I was thinking of making some tea and a little food before I turn in for the night." Does my voice seem as loud to him as it does to me? It can't really be helped—the rain still roars on the roof—but suddenly I have no idea what the right volume is, or whether I'm using it. "I know you said you're not hungry, but would you like to sit in the kitchen while I do that?"

He rolls his shoulders, looking uncomfortable. "I would be happy to help."

I wave this off. "That isn't necessary. Come sit and keep me company." The moment the words leave me I question them. How very...bossy of me. Clearing my throat, I shake off the unsettled nerves and stop questioning myself. "If you'd like," I add to soften my demeanor. Our eyes catch then, and my heart does the same little torturous flip. Ripping my gaze from his I lead the way.

The wolf shifter moves his pack to the door, where it won't be underfoot, and follows me into the kitchen. I put the kettle over the fire and chop up the potato. Then I move on to some vegetables I grew the day before last and tip them into a pot with beans and broth and some meat I had under a preservation spell. On a stormy night like tonight the kitchen witch in me demands a hearty soup.

Smugly I wonder if the smell of the soup will tempt him to eat. He's already denied me twice and a third time won't do.

After all I feel a desire to feed him. To offer him warmth and comfort. My mind drifts and I quickly shut down the thoughts that come.

The shifter accepts a seat at the kitchen table and a cup of tea, sipping it slowly while I move around the kitchen. His large hand around the delicate porcelain saucer forces my lips to pull into a smirk. I have to make an effort to keep my hands steady. I am not embarrassed about cooking—the moons know I have been the only one to cook for myself for the last three years—but I can feel his eyes on me. As the spices are added I ask them to nourish our bodies. I speak more to the soup itself, in my head, than I do to the company I currently keep.

I don't know how to start a conversation. Every time my lips part, my breath seems to leave. As if it rushed out of me and left the words themselves behind. I saw how his eyes went wide when he saw me before. I can feel the heat in his glances. He finds me interesting, and I like the way he looks at me. I more than like it.

The soup bubbles in the pot, and I lean over it, the strangest feeling in my chest.

Is it hope?

Is it something more?

Should I feel this way, when I am meant to be alone?

The questions pile up as I ladle out two bountiful bowls of soup.

The storm is the loudest part of the meal. The soldier tries to ask a few questions about the cottage and the storm, and I tell him that I have lived here nearly all my life, and I have never seen a storm this strong come through. I can barely look at him while we speak. *What has come over me?*

Otherwise, we focus on eating the stew by candlelight. My smile grows with the small groan of satisfaction as he eats. An urge to tease him for denying his hunger at first threatens to spill from my lips. But I keep them shut, merely admiring the roughness of his hands as he eats.

When the stew is gone and we've shared a small loaf of buttered bread to wipe the bowls of every drop, I show him to the small bathing room in one corner of the cottage. It only takes a wave of my hand to fill the bathing tub with hot water. I don't miss the way his shoulders straighten as I wave my hand. How he pays attention to my every movement.

He's intrigued and I love that. I, too, find myself intrigued.

He accepts a small stack of towels and wash-cloths with an expression of mild surprise on his face, then shuts himself in. I stand with my back to the closed door, hand on my racing heart, wondering what he looks like in the nude. The moment I catch myself wondering I roll my eyes at myself.

I do not listen outside the door. Even if I wanted to, I could not hear sloshing water in the tub over the storm. He is a temporary guest, of extreme sexual attraction, but a guest nonetheless.

A little while later, he steps out into the firelight with the towels wrapped around his waist, and I spin around averting my eyes but it's of no use. My mouth waters and my pulse quickens: the view is forever etched into my memory.

I don't want to look away, but the glimpse of chiseled abs and corded muscle over every inch of him made my face flame hotter than I thought it could get. Absent-mindedly, I snatch some crystals from my worktable and pretend to concentrate on rearranging them. I *think* I hear some movement near his pack.

When I straighten up again, he has returned, and is wearing a pair of trousers and what looks to be a clean shirt. Better for my racing heart, but I don't think the color of my face has returned to normal just yet.

"Is there anything else you need?" I look him in the eyes when I say it, though the question feels dangerously close to inviting him into my bed. My voice is a little tight, a little higher pitched than I'd like.

He shakes his head, a noticeable smirk making his handsome face look even more tempting. "Thank you." The rough tone of his voice seems to connect directly to my clit. Oh the moon plays a deadly trick this evening. I shut down all racing thoughts and tell him calmly, "I think I'll ready myself for bed."

The soldier nods, then goes back to the kitchen table and sits while I head to the bathing room.

My hands have never shaken so much from changing into my nightgown and splashing water onto my face. Gripping the handles of the faucet I whisper internally to myself, *it's only one night.*

It is *probably* one night. All the soldier needs is a charge in his crystals, and he will be gone again, back to his life. My eyes lift to the mirror and I tell myself I can keep it together for one night. The poor shifter has been through enough.

I focus on being a good hostess, and nothing more than that.

The first thing I do when I step back into the main room is calm the fire. It does not need to burn all night, but a little heat wouldn't hurt. It is cooler out with the rain, and might get cooler as the night goes on.

The soldier stands and watches as I find another spare pillow and a lighter blanket than what's already in the pile on the floor.

"What is this?" he asks when I offer them.

"For your bed." Saying the word *bed* to him feels risky, too. As if I'm attempting to seduce him when I am very much not. The cottage is *so* small. It has seemed so large around me without my coven, and now it feels like I can't breathe without touching him.

Even though we have not touched. I am very aware of such details.

"I have…" he begins, then stops and reaches for the blankets. "Thank you. I'm grateful for your hospitality."

His fingers brush mine as he takes the bedding, and goosebumps cover my body. Shivers run down my spine and instantly my nipples harden. It was only a moment of heat, but so *much* heat. Are shifters always so hot to the touch, or is it him?

"I could put out the fire," I offer, with my bottom

lip dropped just slightly and unable to be brought back up into place.

He raises one eyebrow, looking into my eyes. "If that would make you more comfortable."

"I thought you might be more comfortable. If you are too warm—"

"I will be fine," he says, before I can finish. "I am well in fact." His tone is low with his last statement. Low enough to bring my thoughts back to where they should not be, at the memory of him in a towel.

"I'm…glad to hear it." More heat on my face, as if the cottage might light ablaze just like the logs in the fireplace. "I will… I am tired. I will go to bed now."

He nods and begins to turn away, but stops and faces me again.

"My name is Ryker." He holds out a big, calloused hand to me. "I thought you should know that."

My body freezes. *Ryker.*

I take his hand, holding my breath for a few seconds at how *powerful* his grip promises to be, though his touch is gentle—extremely careful.

"Idalis."

"Idalis," he repeats. The rain covers most of the softness in his voice, but not all of it. "I'm pleased to meet you."

I'm not sure if he intends it to be so, but the way

he speaks is seductive. With a smile and a blush, I pull my hand away.

The cottage, which seemed like far more room than I would ever need before this evening, gets closer still. Every other night before this, when I lay down in my bed, the main room seemed to be miles long.

It is not miles long anymore. Ryker arranges his bed at the foot of mine, out of the strongest heat from the fireplace, and stretches out as if he's used to sleeping on the floor. All I can hear is the blood rushing in my ears from my pounding heart.

Even in his human form, he is so obviously *strong*. I stare at the ceiling and press my back to the mattress, so I don't sit up and stare at him. My eyes stay wide and although sleep begs me to give in, there is no way I possibly could. My mind races with so many thoughts, many of which are sinful. But others, more logical and terrifying.

The rain drums and drums on the roof, and I have the sense the drops are coming through and landing on my blankets and my clothes. Each one is a cool prickle of doubt.

I do not trust other beings. My coven *died* at the hands of other beings because they'd felt it necessary to fight in the war. A wolf shifter—and a soldier, no less—is no less of a danger to me than the trolls who killed my sisters.

What was I thinking, letting him stay for the night? Why did I hand him a stack of blankets and let him lie down at the foot of my bed? He is practically on top of me.

No, he is not. I cannot fathom what the weight of all those muscles would feel like if he were stretched out over me instead of on the floor.

Or perhaps I *can* fathom it.

I turn over on my side and squeeze my eyes shut tight, trying not to imagine it. He was able to enter, and he sleeps atop an enchanted quilt. I am safe and the moons protect me. I know this and with those thoughts, I let go of my worries.

I force myself to relax and inhale deeply. There's certainly more *energy* in the cottage. All he's doing is lying on his makeshift bed, but power ripples off him.

Power, but not a threat.

Not to me.

I push myself up on one elbow to steal a glance at him. After a few moments, he turns over and stretches before settling down again.

I lower myself back to my pillow, feeling…off. I don't like that he is left to be uncomfortable. I know he is a powerful wolf shifter and a soldier, but I saw how he shifted on the blanket, clearly trying to find a better position for his body.

Sleep evades me.

The soldier makes no move to get up from the bed or to come to mine. He does not leap up and growl. He lies there, and all he seems to do whenever I check on him is breathe.

After what feels like hours of sleeplessness, I can tell he is not sleeping, either.

No matter how many times I tell myself it is all right, sleep will not come. I spend what feels like hours relaxing the muscles in my body bit by bit and counting up to a hundred and back down to one. My eyes burn from the late hour. I can't drift off.

I'm awake so long that the storm tapers off to a downpour, and then to a light rain, and then to a shower that comes and goes. I imagine that I will fall asleep before the rain stops completely, but I find myself listening for the next set of drops, listening and listening and *still* awake.

His breaths are deep and even, but they are too purposeful for him to be truly asleep. I stretch my legs under the covers, trying to work out some of the restlessness.

Stretching does not dispel any of the fidgety feeling, which seems to be everywhere in my body. Even though we are both pretending to sleep—or at least rest—the tension only thickens in the silence. It makes the cottage even hotter than the fire, and without the cooling effect of the rain, the temperature becomes too much.

I wave my hand at the fireplace and send a cool breeze through the cottage.

The soldier lets out a gentle sigh of satisfaction. I let one out as well.

It's still not enough to send me to sleep.

My thoughts circle in my head as the night drags on. I cannot stop thinking of the soldier. I cannot stop listening to his breathing. He is awake. I am awake. We're both awake.

I fall into a pattern, checking to see if he is awake, then noticing he is, then noticing how impossible it is to sleep.

The walls of the cottage draw closer every time I exhale. At the foot of the bed, Ryker turns over a second time, then a third.

After a long time, I think his breathing has settled into real sleep.

I cannot lie here anymore, so I swing my legs out of the bed and tiptoe silently past him, holding my nightgown up so that it does not accidentally brush against his leg and wake him.

In the kitchen, I stand by the window and smooth my hands over my hair, breathing deep.

It's still very dark outside. That could be because of the clouds, or just because it's late, but either way, it soothes me. I cannot see my moon from where I'm standing, but I know she's in the sky.

Maybe I was not able to summon Ryker's portal because it has been so long since I cast in the presence of anyone else.

Without thinking, almost as if I am in a dream, I choose a few crystals from the windowsill and set them in a small triangle. It will not be *his* portal, but if I could summon *a* portal, I could begin to understand why it did not work the first time.

I gather my thoughts and intentions, then ease power into the group of crystals, calling for a portal to come to me.

No portal appears. Not even the hint of one. A morbid unease settles through me. I cannot remember a time when magic has left my side. And now…it fails to open a portal. When I need it most.

I try twice more. All the while holding my breath.

One more try, and I let my hands fall to my sides, breathing hard, fear and dread cold in my stomach.

He's trapped here.

I'm trapped here with him. A true fear of this man being trapped here consumes me. Without a portal he would have to travel on foot either north or south, and both directions are unsafe. Why would fate do this? Trap him here? Why would fate take away my magic?

Swallowing thickly I stare outside at the storm and I know it to be the cause. It must be and it cannot last. With a flick of my fingers I light a candle and raise my hand to the flame, feeling the energy that exists between the heat and my palm. As the thunder cracks through the sky, a chill settles in the space, and as the storm is quieted, the warmth grows.

It is the storm. There is no doubt that once it's passed, magic between spaces will be restored. It must be so. My confidence grows as lightning crashes down and the flame of the fire reacts.

Once the storm passes, I am sure the portals will be restored. With a steadying breath, I convince myself of it.

With the heat at my palm, I wonder how long that may be.

What if I just crawled into Ryker's makeshift bed? What if I warmed myself by his body? Would that solve the problem?

My face sears hot at the thought. *Where did that come from? Does he have some hold over me?*

I blow out my next breath, straighten up, and cross the cottage so I may try to sleep once more, but his hazel eyes catch me in the dead of night.

He is watching me, wide awake.

I startle backward, my hand flying to my throat. Only after I've recovered from a minor heart attack, I speak. "I thought you were asleep," I gasp. "You do not have to pretend to sleep."

He looks at me, his eyes somehow catching the last of the light from the fire's ember. "I didn't mean to alarm you... I couldn't sleep."

*S*he's beautifully awkward. Out of place in her own home. She blushes when she peers at me over her shoulder...as if I wouldn't notice her stolen glances. She clears her throat in this adorable dainty way and seems as if she'll say something, but words fail her. This all-powerful witch that so many fear is no doubt potent with her magic, but she is more of a prey than a hunter. My wolf is tempted and yet sated merely in her presence.

It's obvious that I get to her and I enjoy knowing that fact. Idalis peers down at me, appearing inno-cent with her wide doe eyes and almost delicate in the waning firelight. Her fingers flutter at her throat as if she wants to drop her hand and look stoic but can't.

"You didn't alarm me," she lies. Again she clears her throat in a way that's cute. I never thought that was possible before laying eyes on her. "I wasn't alarmed. I only thought you were sleeping."

"You weren't sleeping either." My response comes with a casual tone, easy and as if unimportant although every nerve ending in my body stands on edge just from talking to her. Just from being up in the late hours with sleep at our fingertips…just as close as the bed is. My cock hardens at the thought of taking her to bed and truly exhausting ourselves how desire intends. Now I find myself clearing my throat and attempting to rid my mind of the image lest the witch finds out my sordid thoughts. I must be a gentleman.

"No." Finally, she lowers her hand, only to clasp it with her other hand. "No, I couldn't sleep, so I thought I would try to cast a portal." Disappointment lingers in her tone, and I wish it didn't. I have no desire for her to create a portal tonight.

I thought that is what she might be doing, though I could not tell with her back turned.

"Did it work?" I question without hinting at my hope that it failed.

"It didn't," she answers, shaking her head and pursing her lips.

My gaze lingers over the curves of her nightgown, the hem well within my reach; another level of hardship. Idalis' scent is sweet, like fresh flowers and a sugary confection that I cannot name. I want to grab the hem of her nightgown and pull her down to the blanket with me. I could suckle the curve of her delicate neck until the worried look disappears from her face, replaced with want and ecstasy. I could spread her thighs and taste her there until I found where all that sweetness comes from. I could make her moan out my name and—

"I'm sorry if I woke you," she says quickly, thankfully interrupting my inappropriate thoughts, then steps around me and pads to her bed.

"You didn't and it's alright," I manage, my throat tight and tense.

The blankets lift, then fall, sending a soft breeze of her scent toward me. *Fucking hell.*

My cock throbs with the torture of her being so close and yet untouchable. She doesn't trust me. I don't trust her. This witch has powers like I have never encountered before, and her wariness is salt in her scent.

What does she think of me? What does she think I will do to her?

Is she afraid that I might *claim* her?

I huff a humorless laugh at the thought, keeping the sound under my breath, and fold my arm under my head. I know not what's come over me only that I crave her more than I have ever craved another. I am surely spellbound and desperate to resist. Time ticks with the thoughts becoming more and more vivid, agonizingly slow.

Idalis doesn't sleep, either. I can feel her there, lying in her bed with her heart racing, mere feet from where I lie.

My mouth waters for the rest of the night. My cock never softens. I want her more with every heartbeat.

Perhaps I should have taken my chances in the forest last night, or started the journey back to my lands, but with us both awake and waiting for the other to speak, or move, or—

Something else.

It's torture.

She never speaks. Idalis is determined to lie as still as she can, it seems. She does so until the sun comes up.

When enough light sneaks in around her shutters, Idalis quietly climbs out of her bed and walks purposefully across the cottage to the bathing room. When she comes out, she is dressed again—a dark green dress that looks as if it was woven from the land around her. A pattern of wildflowers is embroidered at the hem and the cuffs of the sleeves. She eyes me and when our gazes catch, she offers me a simper and another blush then looks away. My head falls back and my eyes close from the vision she is. I'm forced to suppress a growl of satisfaction. She reaches up to her hair to tie it in a low bun at her neck, and the sight makes my wolf howl mournfully. He longs to be allowed to touch her. He yearns to be allowed to bury his nose in the nape of her neck and breathe her in.

"The storm still brews… I'll make tea," she says, without looking at me. "I thought you would like some, but if you do not—"

"I would love a cup." I get to my feet quickly, trying to adjust myself subtly. "Thank you." It's then that the need to sleep truly hits me as I stand. I've gone days without sleep before, but this is different. The warmth and comfort teases me just as the sight of the witch does.

Idalis goes into the kitchen nook. I make a short

stop at my pack and shut myself in the bathing room.

Splashing cold water on my face does nothing to relieve the intense hard-on I have nor does it rid the burning of my eyes needing rest. With both hands gripping the edge of the vanity, I drop my head down to stare at the offending erection. Fucking hell. What this woman does to me.

I wrap my fist around it, wanting more than anything to give in to the lust raging in my blood. Just to be past it all.

Would she know?

That's the thought that makes me let go of my cock like it burned me. I shove my cock back into my clothes, gritting my teeth and thinking of raw blisters and lethal battle wounds to distract myself.

If Idalis can sense me stroking my cock to thoughts of her, then there is no chance she will help me recharge the crystals and summon the portal. No chance at all. The lone woman would kick me out, I'd imagine.

It is one thing to become stranded in a strange land while I have been sent on a mission. It is another thing to actively prolong my stay.

Both of us seem to be on our best behavior when I step out of the bathing room. We have a quiet, polite breakfast of tea and toast with jam, then Idalis seats herself at her worktable, and I take some of the crystals out of my pack and carry them out to charge under what little sun peeks from the storm clouds. The rain is a mere sprinkle now.

The heavy clouds that sat over the cottage for hours yesterday are gone, and the gray wisps they left behind are beginning to break up and let the sun through. Perhaps once the storm has passed, the portal will work.

I go over to the oven—it is well-made of sturdy stone—and arrange the smaller crystals, then hold up the one that is still humming so I can call my commander and give him an update.

Jorge's face appears in the facet. It wobbles for a few beats, then resolves into sharper clarity than it had in the dark under the trees.

"Ryker. Can you hear me?"

"I can." I answer. "I've found the witch, and she offered me shelter but cannot open the portal." Jorge's slight raise of his eyebrow doesn't go unnoticed, and I wonder if it's her hospitality or her lack of ability that gives him pause. "Do you have news of the portal?"

He shakes his head with a grimace. "From what we can tell, all the portals in the entire territory are down. It's as if there's been a cloak thrown over the area."

"All across this land?"

"Yes," he confirms. "None of the portals will open, and we can't open one to come to you." It's surprising how dread doesn't come with his words. Left alone in between enemy territory and at the mercy of the witch…

"All right." I try not to let the relief I can't explain show on my face. "Perhaps once the rain has cleared…if not I will find my way back alone."

"That's not an option, Ryker. It's too dangerous for you to go alone."

My jaw clenches and I don't immediately respond. I'm aware of the danger but I cannot stay here forever.

"Is there a chance this could be the witch's doing?" Jorge asks, his eyes distant, like he has been thinking this problem over all night, just as I have.

"I don't think so," I answer.

"No?"

"Not at all. She doesn't want me here." My wolf aches at the thought, curling up around a wounded spot in the center of him, as if he had actually been clawed open or cut with a weapon of sharpened steel. The tightness in my chest is shocking. I add, ignoring the wave of emotion, "She attempted to make a portal last night. Without success."

Jorge ruffles a hand through his hair and looks past the crystal. I wonder what he sees on the other side, and would ask if I didn't know this expression to mean he is thinking over the plan going forward.

"Perhaps," he muses, after a minute. "It's necessary to give fate time to heal whatever ails the territory. The storm may be a cloak itself. Let us let it pass." His eyes meet mine in the reflection of the crystal, though his image wavers a little, as if it is caught in a strong wind. "If the trouble does not wane, we will come to you one way or another."

I don't expect to feel another wave of relief at Jorge's words, but I do. Comfort at the thought of being alone with Idalis. My curious little witch. My gaze drops slightly at the thought.

My little witch who doesn't wish to spend more time with me. If she could have, she would have sent me through a portal of her own making last night.

"But the wedding," Jorge continues, and a growl catches in my throat. The *wedding*. I had intended to trade my service in gathering the florals in exchange for being excused from attending the ceremony. "You cannot miss it. We will recover you before then."

I nod in understanding. "Yes, sir. I'll stay here until it is safe to leave," I tell Jorge firmly, as if I am agreeing with him, and end the call as soon as he nods at me so that we cannot discuss the wedding anymore.

As his face fades away, the breeze carries a heady floral scent to me, and my body hums with a new awareness of Idalis.

She's behind me.

I gather the crystals in my hands first, then turn to face her. My shoulders straight and at attention.

"My commander wishes for me to stay here," I repeat, because I think she has been listening for a minute or two. "So long, of course, as you will have me." I swallow thickly as I catch sight of her. My breath leaves me. She is a vision with an umbrella held above her and the rain falling gently around her.

Idalis watches me, the hem of her dress moving in the breeze. Then her stormy eyes lift from my face to the skies, which are beginning to clear, the clouds slowly rolling up into a bundle somewhere out of sight. I find myself wishing it wouldn't go. I'd prefer to stay here for as long as she'll have me. However she'd like me, in fact.

Again desire forces me to stifle a groan. This is a

need like I've never felt before. It didn't only over-whelm me this morning, when the scent of her sent me running to the bathing room to fist my own cock. The urge is back, and stronger than ever.

I exhale through my nose and scan the open land around us. The mud is on its way to drying, but it will be some time before it is back to how it was before the rain came.

"The moon is nearly full," Idalis mentions, her full lips staying parted at the last word, tempting me, her eyes returning to mine. "Do you have control of your wolf?"

Your wolf. The manner in which she speaks is haunting in a beautiful way.

"Of course." This is true, for the moment, but my wolf pushes against me from the inside, desperate for control. He wants to have free rein over the body we share and the ability to get closer to Idalis. To nip at her and discover her submissive side. I long for such things as well. To have her writhing under me in complete submission.

She narrows her eyes, peering up at me through thick lashes, and even her mild suspicion makes my cock jerk with desire. Yes, of course, I would rather have her look at me with the same want I feel, but the way she *doubts* me and my wolf—

It's almost playful with curiosity. It's almost as if she knows me well enough to know that my wolf is a hunter. Though I keep him in check, I'm also extremely sensitive to his wishes.

It seems like she may say something but stops herself yet again before changing the subject. "Did you sleep last night? Even for a short time?"

"No. But neither did you."

Idalis lifts her chin with a soft sound of indignation, then begins to stroll to the cottage. She peers over her shoulder as if to tell me to follow. Like I'm some sort of puppy she can command to follow. It's fucking intoxicating how she toys with me. Puppy or not, she's aware I'll follow. It is not far at all, but she takes her time with it. I slip my crystals into my pocket and fall into step beside her. During our short journey, the wind blows warmly through my hair and the sun peeks out from behind the clouds, bathing the grass in light and making the raindrops that still cling to it glisten.

I can imagine how it would be to live here. The land surrounding this cottage is quiet and peaceful, unless there is a heavy rainstorm, and even then, there is shelter and warmth and a gorgeous witch. I wouldn't mind spending hours walking by her side. Following her as she wishes.

She opens the door to the cottage and steps inside. My eyes take some time to adjust to the changed light. At first, the cottage seems dim—almost dark—but finally I can see that it is not. The sun shines in through the windows whenever the clouds let it through.

She pauses again where my blankets are still arranged on the floor at the foot of her bed.

"Perhaps you should rest now," she suggests, her voice low and suggestive, and then she lifts her hand and waves at my face.

I am lightheaded in an instant. Is that because all the blood has rushed to my cock? As soon as the thought comes to my mind, I know it is not true, and I jerk backward, Jorge's suggestion that this is the witch's doing coming back to me with a thunderous warning.

"Do not put a spell on me, witch," I murmur the words at her, letting the threatening growl of my wolf out in full force, but she does not flinch.

"Come to me." Her voice is melodic, soothing, and her gaze never leaves mine. Idalis reaches out her palm to me, offering her wrist and I swear I can hear her heart beat with mine. My body responds to her. It's like I'm walking in a dream. It cannot be more than a few steps to where she stands, her hand still extended. I put my hand in hers, my wolf nearly whining with satisfaction.

My knees start to bend when I reach my blankets, but Idalis guides me past them to her bed. *Fuck yes.*

I'm used to sleeping rough, but the sight of the bed makes me ache for it. I cannot resist the temptation. With a flick of her other hand, Idalis pulls back the covers, and I sink down into the mattress without even a whine of protest. My head lands on the pillow, and I let out a groan.

Why am I so weak? Why can I not stand up to her magic?

Idalis strokes her fingers lightly through my hair, and this time, the purr of a growl from my wolf escapes out of my mouth. It roughly vibrates up my chest.

I think I see her smile, but I cannot be sure, because my eyes are too heavy to keep open. She is blurrier, and blurrier, and then it is dark. And in the darkness there is comfort and warmth and a peace I've never known.

"I should not do this," I mumble. My orders were not to *sleep.* They were not to take the witch's bed and succumb to her magic. They were to—

In this moment, I cannot remember.

I'm fucking tired.

My body is exhausted from the search for the witch and her cottage and from the attempts to summon the portal and from a long, sleepless night spent listening to the rustle of her body on these same sheets.

The bed smells of her, and only of her. No one else has ever slept here. I know it in the marrow of my bones. I nestle deeper into the bedding in spite of myself. Idalis's fingers are still in my hair. Her nails scratch lightly at my scalp, and another *loud* groan of gratification slips between my lips and fills the space between us.

"See?" There is fondness in her voice. Perhaps a bit of amusement. When she tugs the blankets up over me, there is nothing I can do to stop myself from settling in. It feels too comforting and too peaceful. I do not think I have ever felt this relaxed before. "You'll rest," she murmurs. "And perhaps then whatever has come over this land will pass."

With her lips at the shell of my ear, and her warmth so close, sleep takes me under.

IDALIS

he desire that clings to me is tempting. It scares me in ways I would never admit. I shouldn't do it, but I can't tear myself away from Ryker in my bed. I don't know what's come over me. It cannot be a simple curiosity. There's a pull to him. A desire like none I've felt before.

I fear if I were to whisper the confession, everything in my life would change. Goosebumps travel down my arms... Confirmation.

All it took was a wish for his body to know comfort and for safety to surround him. That there was no need to fight his needs. My lips tick up into a smirk remembering how he fought. How he called me a witch. I love it. I've never felt such desire from another calling me by such a name.

For some reason, the word on his lips is sinful and divine all at once. It's unfair, though, that he sees me in such a light when him speaking anything at all to me seems to be a spell of its own. His roughly spoken words and deep baritone voice draws me to him in a way that's undeniable.

He let himself relax onto the mattress as if he has not felt a comfortable bed underneath him before. Perhaps that's true. We have not spoken about anything but the portal, and ever so briefly the flowers he was collecting for a wedding. I'm terrified to know more about him, to let myself fall in obsession with this man. I could hardly look at him this morning, I felt so flushed, so wanton, so unlike myself. And then he took that call on his crystal, which piqued my interest.

I let my thoughts wander to his small collection of crystals, telling myself I am forgetting that my fingers are in his hair while I absently keep stroking through it. His dark hair, clean and dry, is softer than I would have expected, and he seems to relish the feeling, even while he is asleep. I wonder what comfort he's felt before. At the thought, I become jealous. Once again, something I've not felt before. My hands still and I place them in my lap, keeping my hands and thoughts to myself.

How is it that those crystals—the ones he used to make contact with the man who must have been his commander—still hold a charge when mine did not work to summon a portal? Something about that is off-balance. Whatever has dampened the power of the crystals across my land should have affected all of them, yet...

It did not. It's only the portal that's unable to work. All other magic works. I don't understand, and in the back of my mind I am reminded of what my elders told me long ago: *it's not for us to understand, it's for us to accept and be grateful.*

It is a rare day that my intuition is so very quiet. Although it is even more rare that my mind is preoccupied with thoughts of another. Absentmindedly, I toy with the small charm on my necklace. It's a carved obsidian, a stone for protection, in the shape of the moon. I've never felt compelled to take the necklace off, but in his presence, I feel as though I don't need it. I imagine I don't need to wear a thing in front of him.

Heat flushes up my neck and cheeks. My word, what has come over me?

The sharp lines of his strong jaw and rough stubble tempt me. His stiff muscular arms and chiseled chest tempt me.

Everything about him tempts me. I've never found a mortal so enticing. He seduces every part of me. I want to know what it would feel like when his lips touch mine. I want to know what it would feel like to lie on the bed next to him. To fall asleep next to him and dream next to him. To listen to rain on the roof next to him.

Would I even notice rain on the roof if I were in bed with him?

Probably not.

Although—perhaps it is *because* Ryker is not mortal that I find him so enticing. As a wolf-shifter, he is decidedly not a human man. He is so much more.

My fingers linger a few inches above his shoulder. I cannot help myself—I readjust the blankets just so I can feel the heat of him for a heartbeat or two.

Then I turn away from the bed and go to my worktable, breathing deep and slow to try to quench the fire of my...

Curiosity.

I cannot lie to myself. It is not only curiosity. It is an intense desire. I want to know him because I want to...

Have him. I would like for him to be mine. Even if just for a taste.

I would like to be his. If for no other reason than for the memory to exist.

I exhale sharply and fold my hands together, running through several incantations to the moon in my head. I call on her for wisdom and empathy to know why these thoughts plague me. I call on her for calm and peace of mind. I call on her to give me clarity so that I can understand what has happened to the magic here.

I cannot be having these kinds of thoughts! They cannot come to me so easily! I live in solitude because it is the only safe way to live, not because I was waiting for the perfect wolf shifter to come pleading for shelter in the middle of a thunderstorm.

With several deep breaths, I don't suddenly find an answer to the problem of Ryker's portal, but my mind *does* clear.

I feel a pull toward Ryker. With my mind settled —whether by the grace of the moon or from my own efforts or both—that is the one sensation that stands out above all others. It is almost a physical pull, like a string tugging at my waist, trying to pull me back to him.

And then, I suppose, it would have me climb into

the bed. Nap the day away? Press myself closer to him in my sleep? Reach for him in my dreams?

Allow my lips to touch his and see what sensations come over me?

I will not be doing that. Not right now.

It must be my prolonged loneliness that's making me think this way. With such temptation and curiosity.

Ryker's handsome, powerful, and strong. Much stronger than a mortal man.

Above all, he is trustworthy. He has stayed in my cottage for an entire night, longer than anyone has in years, and he has not made a single move to assert dominance over me.

Although that very thought sparks a different kind of want. One I shove to the back of my mind.

Shoulders back, I return to one of the shelves by my worktable and find my worn, beloved tarot cards.

The cards are soft and pliable from having been shuffled between palms hundreds and hundreds of times. As I gently let them slide against one another, I center my mind on them. On the smooth, slippery feel of the cardstock. On the wisdom they hold. On the answers I'm seeking.

I meditate on the events of the past day.

What change in the world around me brought on the storm? Did that force also inspire the pull I feel toward Ryker? I think of him most of all, dwelling on how open his expression is when he's sleeping and the long frame of his body on my bed and the sound of his breathing.

I need these things to be clearly communicated to the cards, so I pace quietly around the cottage, turning all of it over in my mind—but especially Ryker. The soft sound of his steps. The light grumble in his throat when he contemplates. The sharpness of his eyes as our glances catch one another. The little details that make him who he is, that's what I focus on as I hold the cards and absently shuffle them.

Every time I make another circuit of the room, I cannot help letting my gaze linger on him.

The afternoon light from outside caresses his skin as if it wants to touch him as much as I do. He sleeps as if he is sure of his safety here, deep within the peace of the spell I put on him. He's turned over onto his back and flung out both arms, taking all the space he can on the bed.

Surely I would only fit if he were holding me.

With the thought shocking me to my core, I return to the cards.

What brought you here? I ask, not of him, but of the cards and the moons. There's a simple answer to this question, but I already know it. I want the cards to show me the hidden reasons that Ryker—who is not from this land and was sent here by his commander —truly came here. Why did fate send him here? Why truly, with the meaning of life and purpose has this man come to my door?

When the cards are sated from shuffling and warm in my hands, I sit down at my worktable and clear a space. I keep Ryker at the forefront of my mind, held in concentration, asking the cards over and over to respond to him. To show me the inner truth of the most beautiful man who has ever crossed my threshold.

Open my eyes, I request of the cards. *Show me the things I cannot know. Help me to understand the will of the fates.*

One by one, I draw four cards and lay them out on the table.

The first card is the Two of Cups.

The second card is the Lovers.

The third card is the King of Pentacles.

The fourth card is the Queen of Pentacles.

I look at the cards in their neat spread before me, my heart racing.

The lovers on its own would have given me a shock, but along with the King *and* Queen of Pentacles? What could the cards be referring to if *not* me and Ryker?

But we are not lovers.

"We are not," I tell the cards in a breathless whisper as my heart races. Even the Two of Cups echoes the message of the Lovers card. My questions catch in the back of my throat. This desire I feel, it is not temporary. This shifter is for me. But shifters have mates. Surely, I cannot be his lover.

The cards stare back up at me. They could represent the future or the past as well. Perhaps another lifetime. A star-crossed lover maybe?

The King and Queen of Pentacles together represent...

Well, it represents power. Two forms of power. Both outward strength and inner balance. As a pair, they represent a nurturing emotional core and material abundance.

In other words...a marriage. Although a chill comes over me. I think of the royal wedding. Maybe it doesn't refer to us after all. Maybe it's the prince and princess that brought us here like this.

I steal a glance at Ryker.

He's still deeply asleep. My pounding heart didn't

wake him, then. I take a few deep breaths in case his wolf's senses are honed enough to hear my pulse going faster and faster.

My heart doesn't want to slow down. Even the Two of Cups is another card that clearly represents a *pair.* At its best, the Two of Cups is about harmony. Every card I've pulled is either half of a fated pair or a pair in and of itself.

But, I think at the cards, *I'm not part of a pair. He is only a temporary guest, and he did not come here to find a match. He came here to gather flowers for a wedding.*

My conflicting thoughts war in my mind.

A wedding is yet another representation of a harmonious pair. The wedded couple is literally at the center of the ceremony.

I close my eyes and refocus. There is more on the horizon than weddings.

Ryker will leave. Charging his crystals, opening a portal, and going back home are the reasons he's here. He doesn't have any other business with me, as far as I know, and I do not have any other business with him. If it weren't for the storm, we might not have crossed paths at all.

We did, though, and now our lives are entwined for a time.

Eyes still closed, I slide a card off the deck and onto an empty stretch of the table.

When I open my eyes, I am confronted with Death. My body stills as a coldness comes over me. Chills run down my spine, and layer after layer of goosebumps follow.

It takes a few moments for me to process what I am looking at. Of course, it is the Death card—that much is clear. But it is reversed.

Death, reversed.

Death is the end. Death reversed is rebirth and renewal. The end of what exactly? Although deep in the marrow of my bones, I know exactly what it's referring to. I know what must end although I do not wish it to be so.

I glance at him again, half-expecting to find him watching me, alert and awake.

He's not. He has turned over onto his side, and his chest rises and falls in a slow, dreamy rhythm.

I want so badly to forget the cards and let myself savor the peace and comfort of the cottage as it is right now, with Ryker sleeping in my bed and sun coming through the windows, but I cannot.

My tarot cards have posed questions that demand answers.

That card is the embodiment of change—of

letting go of your old life and stepping into a new one. But when Death is reversed, it usually means that you are resisting the change. Fighting it. But that it is certain. It will come.

Before I ask a particular question that nags in the back of my mind, I cast another spell at Ryker. He was awake all night, and I do not know how long he was traveling before he came to the cottage. He needs as much rest as he can get.

I face the cards once more and close my eyes, allowing myself to acknowledge how fiercely I feel Ryker's presence in my home. I'm aware of every breath he takes, and his masculine scent is everywhere. I notice him more every minute. As afternoon moves on toward evening, time slips away as I grapple with the questions in my mind and the growing sense that I am about to understand some aspect of it, some *fact*, that will change everything.

If that is what is fated to happen, then I will learn to survive in my new reality. I have done it before, and I can do it again.

It is time to be brave and ask the cards directly.

Who is this shifter to me? I ask the cards, keeping my mind open to the possibility that the cards may only be able to hint at such a vague question.

Before I can draw a card, I am drawn to open my eyes.

My gaze immediately snaps to one of the candles on my worktable, which lights the instant my eyes fall on the wick. It hits me at once. All of it coming into focus. I know exactly what happened and as my bottom lip drops, my breath leaves me.

Oh, gods, oh *gods*, it was my fault. This is all my fault.

Because this is the candle I used to cast over the gift for Prince Adom and Princess Charlotte.

What did I write on that candle to cause *all* of this?

I reach for the candle with a shaking hand; I caused this. It is all my fault.

Clarity & Truth Spell

When intuition fails you and you're desperate for answers do the following:

You'll need a purple candle first. Purple for wisdom and psychic abilities. Lapis or clear quartz will work well as a crystal to provide energy. Lapis for truth and spiritual awareness.

Light your candle, write a petition on paper that will burn. Whatever truth you seek, ask for it to reveal itself to you. Hold the crystal in your left hand, the paper with your petition in the right. Stare at your flame, envisioning the light getting brighter and brighter. Your world is filled with bright white light shining down on you. Feel it on your skin. Know that you are surrounded by this light.

Chant the incantation: *The truth comes to me and surrounds me. I know exactly where it is.*

Then burn your petition and have gratitude knowing the clarity and truth will seek you out as you blow out the flame. Put the crystal under your pillow and in your dreams you'll see the truth. So mote it be.

The peace is only disturbed by my shock at such peace. I sleep and sleep, deeper than I have in years. I don't know that I've known comfort like this.

The witch is powerful…but the sleep itself stirred my wolf and his own needs. Several times, I become aware that I'm dreaming. In my dreams, I'm walking across the field outside Idalis's cottage in the early morning, the dew still wet on the grass and the air fresh and clean in my face. In some of the dreams, I have my pack on my back, its weight a comforting presence. In others, I don't have it, and I can tell from the feel of my clothes that they are not my uniform and leather armor.

Sometimes, Idalis walks next to me, a quiet smile

on her beautiful face. She laughs at what I say, though I do not truly understand the words that come out of my mouth. It's a bewitching sound. A sound that soothes the depths of my soul. There is no fighting, no war, only peace with her beside me.

Sometimes, she is not there, and I'm determined to find her. Nothing will stop me from reaching the place where she has gone. I do not have a map, and I do not know where it is, but I know nothing that appears before me will prevent me from finding her again. It may slow me, or hurt me, but it cannot overcome me. The fear is unlike anything I've ever felt before. We must find her. My wolf howls in pain without her.

When I drift closer to wakefulness, the creaking of the cottage surrounds me. The gentle hiss of the wind and the pitter-patter of the rain on the roof. It's a quiet place when the storm settles. Birds cry in the sky as they pass.

Though I am not entirely used to the sounds, none of them alarm me. I'm still so tired that I simply drift off again.

At some point, there is a new heaviness on my body. It covers me like the blankets, and I sink into an even deeper sleep—one in which I do not dream. I am not aware of the world at all.

It is true rest, something I have not experienced since I was a child. I must've rested deeply then—I was a child, after all, and children cannot be kept from their rest. But as an adult and a soldier, there has never been a time when I did not have to keep one ear pricked for approaching danger or the footsteps of a commander or a call to battle. I've *always* been on alert, waiting for orders. My lone wolf scarred but at attention and waiting for purpose. I've spent so long in readiness for the next task set before me that I had forgotten what it was like to rest like this. To feel so complete. To be with her.

The most beautiful witch. Who soothes my soul. Who accompanies my wolf.

Idalis's spell must have been a good one, because even her presence does not pull me from the bed. I never forget that she is there—unless I am in that dreamless sleep—but my wolf is satisfied that she is close, and even he curls up to rest and does not grow impatient.

In one dream, I'm crossing the fields, but Idalis is not with me. Her scent is on the air, strong and pure, and I let my wolf nose it as much as he wants, following his lead on which way to go.

Her cottage is ahead of me, somewhere in the moonlight, and my wolf howls with the joy of an impending hunt. My muscles are warm and loose, and my heart thrums with anticipation. She's there. She's *there*. My mate.

The love, the desire, the need to be beside her… it's all-consuming.

I'm so *sure* of it in the dream. Idalis is my mate, made for me and I her. So mote it be. The dark skies are clear above me, filled with moons and stars, and I can see for miles across the field.

Finally, I see it, there in the distance. The cottage is a dark shadow against the darker tree line, as it was the night of the storm, but light glows from behind the shutters, outlining each window and the door.

The wind stirs, carrying the sound of Idalis's laughter. I adjust my pack on my back. This is one of the dreams where I have it, then. That single touch tells me that it is heavy with the florals, rolled up into bundles. I have collected twice as many as I need for my wedding.

I've gathered the florals for Idalis so that we have abundant power for our ceremony.

A grin spreads across my face, and my heart ticks fast with delight. Yes. Our *wedding*. That's why I have left Idalis in the cottage and roamed the forests of Athica.

Our union is just there. It's so close. I will be there in a matter of minutes, and when I open the door, the scent of my mate will fill my lungs, and her body will fill my arms, and then I'll be able to mark her with a sealing bite on her neck under the full moon. Followed by languid licks and open-mouthed kisses as I fuck her deeply and roughly just how she likes it.

I lengthen my strides, taking up more and more of the land with each step. Nearly running to see her.

I have so many things to say to her. I have so many promises to murmur into her skin.

The cottage stays the same distance away, but I do not break my stride. I move faster and faster until I am almost running—and then I *am* running, my legs burning as I move up gentle slopes in the field and descend the other side.

Still, the cottage does not get closer.

A pinprick of fear digs into the back of my neck, and the hairs on my arms raise in answer. I should be there by now. It never gets closer.

Is this some other spell, or curse? Has the land turned against me? Is it trying to keep me away from her? For I was never meant to find my wolf mate. But she is no wolf, and she is mine. I know it so!

A portal appears in the air ahead of me, open to my homeland on the other side, but I change directions and avoid it, going past. No, no, I cannot leave her!

The storm rages inside of the portal, threatening and striking down lightning as the sky darkens. No! I don't want to leave. Not now. I can't!

"Idalis!" I scream her name but there's no sound.

Idalis's cottage is no closer as I sprint, my lungs aching and sweat pouring down my back. The night air hardly stirs. It is too still. All the land around me is too still. Why didn't I notice before? It is as if I am running through a painting of the land and not the land itself. A land like this should be alive with birds and insects and creatures in the forest, but it makes no sound.

Am I alone here?

I cannot be alone here.

"No," I say aloud to the stillness. "No. This is not real. This is a dream. You cannot keep me from her! She is mine!"

With those words, the land comes to life around me. A nightbird calls from some nearby tree, and a small animal bounds across my path. Idalis's cottage is closer, then closer again, and in a matter of steps I am slowing to a halt by her front door.

I put my hand on the handle and pull.

It swings open, and there she is, standing just inside, a bundle of white cloth in her arms. Her eyes brighten when she sees me, and her face flushes.

"Ryker, my love," she says, and a shudder of sheer arousal goes through me. No one has ever said my name like that before. With such devotion. There's some other magic in it—there must be. It is a claiming, somehow. The air is thick with it. With peace. Even though we are not married yet, there's something in her voice that makes me think we are bound by fate. Meant for me. Mated.

My dream-mind is not surprised by this at all. My dream-mind knows that she is my mate, and always has been. My dream-mind knows that a wedding ceremony is not necessary to tie our souls together, but it is a celebration that means something to Idalis, so we will have one, even though we are already mated. My dream-mind is amused by the idea of a wedding ceremony and enchanted by it, too —not because I have any special fondness for wedding ceremonies, but because I have a special fondness for Idalis, and anything my mate wants, I will give her.

"Mate," I say. It is the only word that comes close to describing this feeling.

"Did you find the florals?" she asks, blushing as she steps closer, hugging the linen to her chest.

"I found them all." I swing the pack off my back and let it rest on the floor at my feet. "I found you."

"Of course you did." She laughs again, an enchanting, sweet sound. "Why wouldn't you have found me? This is our home. I've been here always, waiting for you."

Any uneasiness I felt melts away. What she says is true. It is real. The strange distance before was a trick of the dream and nothing else. We were always meant to be.

"Come here." I reach for her. "I need my mate in my arms."

Idalis offers me a simper, her eyes darkening with her palpable want, and shifts the white cloth she holds into one arm so she can extend her other hand to me.

Her fingers are inches from mine when the color begins to fade. The edges of the dream close in until Idalis's face is all I can see, and then she's gone, too.

I'm back to staring at the darkness behind my eyelids.

This time, I don't immediately sink back to sleep. I lie still on the bed for a few beats, listening. My heart pounds and my body thrums with life. My wolf, content and sated.

The cottage is quiet. No humming. No footsteps. Idalis's scent is still in the air, but this is her home and I am covered in her blankets, so it may not be a sign that she's here.

Cautiously, not trusting what I've dreamed, I stretch my legs out quietly as I open my eyes. I've been sleeping so long that they do not open quickly. I roll each wrist, finding them limber, slow to wake, too.

Then I push myself up. And that's when I see her, my heart beats in a different rhythm.

Idalis has not gone anywhere. She's moved to a seat by the fire, where the light kisses the curves of her face and she is fast asleep, some cards held in her hands atop a knitted blanket.

I watch her for a minute or two, my chest filled with a feeling I cannot name. Her position on the chair by the fire cannot be comfortable. Once that thought has passed through my mind, I cannot spend another second in Idalis's bed.

Quietly so as to not disturb her, I take the cards out of her hands and place them on her worktable. Then I carry Idalis to her bed, place her carefully in the spot I just left, and tuck the covers over her. Her body is soft and warm and my gods, her scent. As I carry her across the room I realize it's the first time I've touched her, although still not skin to skin. So close to heaven. That's what it's like being so close to her.

Idalis stirs, letting out a soft breath, and turns over. She does not wake.

After so much time in bed, I need to move. I go silently to the door and let myself out into the night.

I truly *did* sleep all day. The moon is high in the sky and nearly full. My wolf stirs at the sight of it, coming fully awake himself.

Feeling the need to shift, I leave her side quickly. Out into the darkness, I close the door behind me before shedding my clothes.

It's a relief to shift into my wolf form. To stretch my limbs and allow him to take over. I take a few swift steps, then trot away from the cottage. The world smells different when I am a wolf. I catch the trails of many small woodland creatures who passed through the taller grasses over the last day. Not a mortal soul can be scented. I can smell the differences in patches of soil, and whether it was slightly higher or slightly lower when the rain soaked in. I can smell a den of rabbits somewhere in the forest.

My wolf bounds into a run, streaking through

the night air, his muscles working in perfect coordination, his heart speeding up with the thrill of this new environment, made fresh by the rain. My mate. My mate. My mate. It's all I can think. All he can think. The vigor of his run and the sheer thrill is intoxicating.

There have been times before when I have spent hours and hours in my wolf form, running as far as his powerful body could take me. I plan to let him run now, too, for as long as he needs.

But I haven't yet reached the trees when he makes a sudden turn, streaking back toward Idalis's cottage.

I try to urge him back into the open field, but he resists, snapping at me.

Run, I tell him in the voice of my thoughts. *Run. Stretch. Hunt.*

My mate. She's my mate. My mate.

His whimper outside of the cottage is followed by a howl. A deep need for companionship. A need for her to know. My heart twists in my chest. Doubt creeps in. It was only a dream. I drag myself out of my wolf form and back into my human form, stumbling to a halt at the top of a low rise and heaving in breath after breath. My hand is on the door before my mind can catch up with what my wolf is sure of.

Idalis is still in bed, still asleep, and I cross the main room to the side of her bed feeling like I am dreaming—and like I am wide awake at the same time. The pounding in my chest is all I can hear. I take a few more deep breaths, which are filled with her scent. *That* scent. The scent that called to me, promising a mate. It's a heady feeling.

A *mate*.

I did not take the dream for the truth. Why would I? I have known for most of my life that I would never have a fated mate. No wolf would ever be paired with me.

I pause at the foot of Idalis's bed and look down at her.

She's curled on her side, her head on the pillow, her breathing slow and steady. Gorgeous and peaceful.

My mate. My mate. My mate.

I thought the curse could never be countered. I thought there were no loopholes. No wolf would ever be paired with me, so I would never have a mate. It seemed so simple that it could not possibly be wrong.

And yet the curse *was* wrong. Or it was only right in terms of one aspect of my life, not all the others.

Idalis is my mate.

Chills run down my arms. My dream was the first to try to tell me. My wolf was the second. Now it is my own mind screaming the truth.

And *this* truth cannot be wrong. The way everything shifts inside of me as I lay eyes on her. The way my body begs me to love her. The need I feel to tell her. To nip at her neck and make love to her under the full moon.

I should think this through.

But I cannot tear myself away. I cannot make myself stop staring. I cannot shake off the shock. I do not know when it will ever fade.

I have a fated mate. And she's a witch. *Idalis is my mate.*

It's been a long time since I slept like this. The last time I can recall sleeping so easily, and so soundly, was when my coven was still alive. When I wasn't alone. When there was love in this home.

It was impossible for me to find peace after they died, and it took months for me to sleep more than a few hours at a time at all, and then it was never as restful as it used to be. I wasn't used to being alone, and then, when I became accustomed to it, I grieved that, too. And then even that grief faded into acceptance.

What else could I do? I couldn't bring them back. I couldn't trust a stranger to watch over me. The only safety was in solitude, no matter how much I craved the company of people like my coven.

Eventually, I managed to convince myself that my sleep each night was deep and restful.

Now, as I fall into a vivid dream, I know that it was not. With him here, I am protected. I know this to be true.

I am deeply certain of it, down to my bones. This is a *dream*, thick as honey in my tea.

In my dream, I'm walking in the fields I have called my home for years. I know each dip in the earth and each tree on the horizon. I'm at peace with my fingertips grazing the tall grass and the warmth of the sun soaking into my skin.

I move a few more paces across the lush grass and realize in a blink that these are *not* the same fields that surround my cottage. I know every inch of those fields like the back of my own hand, and this place is different.

Although my heart skips a beat, I do not fear it. I am at home here. Comfortable. It is my waking mind that feels the difference so sharply. The dream-version of me feels nothing out of the ordinary.

I stroll through the fields, in no hurry to get anywhere, pausing often to fill my basket with flowers whose names I do not know. I bend to pick another, then another, and they blow in the breeze, their stems curving gently as the wind moves over them. They seem happy to see me, somehow—they reach their petals toward my fingers and come easily from the earth, content to be gathered. Everything I touch is warmed by the sun.

I straighten from plucking a violet flower and shade my eyes with my hands. Everything about this land—the hills, the wind, the trees in the distance—whispers *welcome home.*

The skyline is not the same. There are unfamiliar mountain peaks and patterns in the trees that do not belong to my forest. The scent I inhale is one I know intimately, yet I have never smelled it before this moment. Before this dream. It is not the scent of my valley in any of the seasons. It is totally new to me, but in this dream I know it so well and find it comforting.

I'm meant to be here. It's missed me so. I was always supposed to be here.

A white cloud moves across the sun, hardly dimming its light.

I become aware of a person next to me. He's nearby in my waking life. In my cottage. And he is at my side in the dream, though I do not turn my head to see his face.

Out of the corner of my vision, his form shifts, becoming larger and more muscled, on four legs, and then he is a man again. He is a wolf shifter, and his scent is on the wind. I know that scent as well as I know the scent of the earth under my feet.

Ryker. My love.

Then this must be Ryker's home. This must be where he traveled from, or where he intends to go one day when he is no longer a soldier.

I marvel at the landscape. At the feel of him beside me. At the sunlight and the mountains and the sky, which is so different from the sky above my cottage...and so similar. There are the moons that remain visible in the daylight. They are in slightly different places in the sky from what I would expect, but I can still find them and name them. Of course, my moon shines down with such happiness. Such blessings that we are together. Tears prick at the back of my eyes.

It is possible that I am seeing Ryker's land as it really is. The dreams of witches are oftentimes visions of the future or glimpses of one's fate. They are not always the imaginings of a mind at rest. This possibility makes my heart race with excitement and anticipation and...delight?

Yes. It is delight I feel. I am delighted in the

dream as well as being deeply content. I want to be happy. I want to be loved. So deeply loved. I didn't realize what was lacking. I didn't know the loss truly until I felt it now.

"Thank you," I say, without turning to face Ryker.

"For what?" he asks. His voice is a deep rumble that seems to come from everywhere at once.

"For watching over me."

He laughs. "How could I not? You are my shelter, my peace, my love… My mate."

"Where is your home?" I ask, but there is no answer from Ryker.

The wind rustles the grasses and the flowers at my feet. It is a stronger wind—too harsh for the flowers. They bend farther, petals coming loose. An uneasy feeling makes my skin prickle with goosebumps. The light changes, growing darker, though it cannot be midday.

"Ryker," I call, forcing myself to stay calm.

"Come home," he says, his voice farther away.

I turn to look for him but only find dark clouds rushing across the sky toward the field where I stand. They're tall, thick clouds, the undersides the color of a cauldron. The rain falls in silvery trails. It will be a heavy rain. Heavy enough to turn the fields to mud and flood the portals.

"Where did you go?" I call into the wind. My voice echoes but I hear nothing else. It snaps against my face. The front edge of the storm is on top of me. It has come on too fast and tears at my clothes, dragging the fabric across my skin.

The sun disappears completely behind the clouds. There's a green tinge to the light. My hair comes out of its braid, and strands whip into my eyes. I turn away from that wind and start walking back toward—

Where? Our home?

There is nothing there but the darkened storm. Thunder rumbles and a loud crack of blinding lightning strikes and wakes me from my dream.

With a racing heart, my body jolts and in the distance there's a gentle click of my front door closing quietly. My breath is stubborn to come and I find my hand over my heart.

My eyes adjust to the light and then I realize I'm in bed, though I do not remember coming here. I recall asking the cards for guidance, and sitting in my chair by the fire, and then…

Nothing. I must have dozed off. More than dozed, really. I must have fallen deeply asleep, because Ryker *must* have brought me to my bed, and I do not remember him lifting me. Slowly my heart calms and the cracking of the fire seems to dim the memory of the dream.

The blankets are warm and doing their best to make me sleep longer, but the guilt twisting in my chest will not let me fall back into the dream. Neither will the thought of Ryker carrying me to bed. I finally push myself upright, rubbing my eyes with one hand to clear the sleep, and there he is. My heart does a faint flip, and a calmness settles around me.

Unlike my dream, he's not hidden in the corner of my eye. Ryker stands near the kitchen table, poised with his sharp features as handsome as ever. The stubble on his jaw only adds to his sex appeal. His gorgeous eyes meet mine, and a shock of heat between us makes me desperate to be free of the blankets. It's dark outside, but inside my cottage, candles flicker to life.

"I have to tell you something," Ryker says as I push my hair back from my face and find a tie on the pillow. I just need it off my neck. I attempt to hide my flush as I pull my hair back and calm my racing heart. His tone is deathly serious, and I don't like what that does to me.

"I need to tell you something, too. It's my fault," I blurt out, my words stumbling out quicker than I'd like. All that time I spent dreaming, and I could have used it to plan how I would tell this truth to Ryker. Instead, I have thrown it out ahead of me, and now I have to hurry to catch up.

Ryker furrows his brow, his eyes narrowing. "What's your fault?"

"I'm the one who—I did this." I gesture at my chest. "I cast a wayward spell. I only had the best of intentions, but I think it's my fault the portal doesn't work."

He crosses the cottage toward me, the floor creaking gently under his weight, and I stand up as tall as I can, bracing for his anger. *I* am the one who trapped him here. *I* am the one who shut down his portal and stopped him from going home.

"I—I will try to undo it." I sidestep Ryker, my arm brushing against his as I rush to my worktable, reaching for the candle I burned to cast the spell for the wedding gifts.

There's nothing left of it. It is down to a stub of wax and a crumbling wick. The tip of my finger barely grazes the wick, and it turns to ash. But even in ash there is intention which means there is magic.

The air in the cottage shifts behind me. I know

without looking that Ryker has drawn closer. I can feel his heat, but he does not touch me.

"Ryker," I bring myself to say. "I'm sor—"

"I believe," he says from behind me. "I am fated to you."

That stops the whirlwind of thoughts in my mind. I turn to face Ryker, forgetting the guilt and the relief and the uncertainty. His eyes hold as much guilt as my heart. Because he believes we are *fated*?

"I'm not a shifter," I barely whisper. My voice sounds breathless even to me, but that is all I can think to reply. I am a *human witch*. Ryker is a wolf shifter. We are opposite beings.

A small, amused smile curves the corner of his lips, just as devilish as charming. "I don't think my wolf cares." The lust inside of me roars to life.

Then I see it—the heat in his eyes, dark and strong and feral, as if his wolf has pressed forward and is crying out to the moon. To *me*. The tension between us intensifies. I feel as if I'm back under the blankets, but the only way to cool this fire would be to take off all my clothes. To let Ryker touch me. To let him *have* me. *Is this why I want him so? Is there some piece of the spell that trapped him because our fate was forced to be?*

"I have never done…such things," I admit, my

voice breaking down to a whisper. My gaze trapped in his. My heart ticks slower, yet faster all the same. It's all too much.

Ryker takes one step closer. "That is fine with me, Idalis."

I force myself to look away. It's all too much. All too sudden. My pulse ticks in my neck. I cannot breathe deeply enough to calm myself. His closeness strips away all the self-control I've maintained in my solitude.

"It's only the moon playing tricks on us." My voice shakes as I say the words, but I offer them anyway, though I do not know why. Perhaps I want him to know he has a way out. Perhaps I want to give him an explanation so that he feels free to leave. Although I desperately want him. This is too good to be true. *He's* too good to be true.

"I have heard…" Ryker slides his hand onto my waist, his touch careful and light, not moving my body at all. "The moon doesn't know how to play tricks, only how to shed light on what we're afraid of."

Chills ripple down my spine, followed by a tingling heat. Want and desire flood every part of me.

Slowly, using all my courage, I turn my face to

Ryker's. When our eyes meet, more heat rushes down my spine, soothing away the nervous chills and breathing air into my lungs.

Ryker's eyes drop to my lips, then burn slowly back to my eyes. *Oh fuck me.* He's more tempting than any dream I've ever had. More handsome than I could have envisioned. More than anything I knew I was ever destined for. *Ryker.*

"Even if it is only a trick, should we not humor the moon?" he asks, his tone teasing. A smirk is forced to my lips.

Yes. *Yes.* We should always humor the moon. My breath hitches as he comes a step closer.

I don't know whether it is Ryker who leans down or me who tilts up on my tiptoes. All I know is that our lips come together, I'm filled with such a sense of wholeness that I gasp and press my whole body closer to his, desperate and wanton in a way I never thought I would be.

With my body pressed to his, I feel *every* part of him.

He is *hard.* All of him is hard, of course, his muscles trained for strength, but his cock is a thick bulge in the front of his trousers, and that realization is like its own flame. Ryker's body is not disappointed to have a mate. Ryker's body *craves* me.

And so does Ryker. A whimper of need escapes my lips at that realization, and I rock myself into him. A gentle growl of desire is my reward. He kisses me deeply, licking and tasting me as he pulls me closer with both hands on my hips. I find his hair and bury my fingers in it, rising up on tiptoe and letting my weight settle in his hands. It does not seem to take any of his strength at all to hold me here.

Lust and desire and primal need cling to us as we cling to each other.

Ryker wraps one of his arms around my waist, and we both sink farther into the kiss like two people who have been starving for touch. I have been starving, I realize. I've been so lonely that I could not recognize my own cravings.

I throw my arms around his neck and suck at his bottom lip, pressing my teeth lightly into the swell of it. He growls, a sound that would have terrified me mere days ago but excites me now. My nipples pebble as pleasure builds in the pit of my stomach. Ryker lifts me fully off the floor, then, and I do not care where he is taking me—I only care about kissing him, and memorizing him, and making him growl again.

I need to feel him, every way I'm able.

After a few steps, Ryker sets me gently onto the bed and crawls over me, his clothes shifting with his bunching muscles. He kisses me again, holding me to the blankets and licking his way down my neck, down and down until he can push the hem of my dress up to my waist, then higher. He lifts me half off the pillows to pull it over my head. Every nerve ending is on fire with need. Every light touch brings desire.

In moments, I am bare to him. And I love it. I need him. I need *this*.

"Idalis," Ryker says, his voice so low it could be an earthquake. He rakes dark eyes over my skin and follows them with his fingers, sliding the pads of his thumbs under the curves of my breasts and over my nipples. I arch on the blankets when he bends to breathe onto the sensitive peaks, and when he licks them—

I lose all sense of time and place. The pleasure is unlike anything I've ever known. He kisses down my belly to the soft flesh between my thighs. The first lap of his tongue over my clit forces me to call out his name. I clench the sheets beneath me as my thighs tremble from the pleasure.

Ryker does not let up. He licks a shaking, shuddering orgasm from me, then seems to go wild for my arousal on his tongue, lapping and sucking and teasing for so long that my thighs begin to shake in a way I cannot stop.

"Fucking delicious," he growls and would lick me again if I did not pull him up from between my thighs, begging as I do it.

"Ryker," I gasp. "Ryker, please. Please. *I need you.*"

Ryker rips his clothes off his body as quickly as possible while kissing over my heated skin. He pushes my thighs apart and I feel a moment of nervousness as he kneels between them. Time slows and all I can hear is our shared breathing.

But then he drags the head of his cock over my clit and down to my opening.

"Oh—" My lips part and I hold my breath with a small whimper.

At this sound he gathers me into his arms and turns us over so I am settled in his lap, his back against the wall. He pulls my face to his and shushes me while he grips my hips and guides me into position. My hands find his chest and I love the touch.

"Whatever pace you need," he tells me. It's obvious he's holding himself back. His breathing chaotic, his gaze sharp, and his eyes nearly gold as I stare deeply into them.

His eyes are filled with wanting. He needs this so

much. I can taste it in the air. I feel no fear when the head of his cock nudges against my opening. I feel only desire. I rock my hips slightly down and the stretch stings with a hint of pain but also pleasure.

"Take me in," Ryker murmurs and guides me down. His lips find the crook of my neck and my head falls back. Slowly, I move. "Ryker," I cry out softly and his lips catch mine.

I gasp at the size of him, and the stretch, and the sensation of my body opening for him. He rubs my clit as I sink down, sending new shocks of pleasure around my hips and down to my toes. I take him slowly because I must, but it feels more and more urgent with every inch that he be as deep inside me as he can get.

Finally, we are skin to skin, and I rock my hips, letting out a desperate moan. My clit brushes against him and I need more. The sensation is so much and still not enough.

"Fuck me, Ryker. Please fuck me."

Ryker growls, full-throated and loud, and helps me ride him, his grip on my hips moving me up and down but mostly closer, grinding us together, chasing his pleasure and mine until I do not think I can come again.

I still as the pleasure builds but he keeps me

moving. The heat grows and my toes curl. I cry out his name as I reach my climax and come undone. He rides through my orgasm, sending me higher and higher. My head thrashes, I don't know if I can take any more but his kisses silence my fears and I come again. Violently. I scream his name against his lips.

Then he pulls me down flush against him, crushes his lips to mine, and comes with a cry that's almost a howl, spilling heat inside me.

I slump against him, panting, and he puts his arms around me. I can feel his pulse where we touch. My heart beating against his.

I do not know how long we rest, silent, before I find the strength to push myself upright and look into Ryker's eyes.

He twitches inside me and—astonishingly— begins to grow hard again.

"Take me again," I beg. Not wanting to think. Only wanting to feel.

Ryker smiles and pumps his hips into me. "As you wish."

This is what it is like, then, to be lost in a mate. The scents of her, the sounds of her, the slide of her lips against mine— every little piece of her is perfect. I would not change a single thing about her. She was made for me and I for her.

I want her just as she is. All my senses sing, almost howling that she is a goddess. My goddess. The most perfect being I will ever touch. My powerful witch.

I want to mark her, too. I want every inch of her marked with my scent so there is not a creature in any land who would mistake her for anything but mine.

My wolf gives a low sound of assent which comes out of my own mouth as well. The moon is nearly full if not there yet. The need to claim my mate is strong.

I kiss the pulse point at the side of Idalis's neck. I kiss the dip of her belly button. I kiss the curve of each thigh. I lick droplets of sweat from her skin. I find every curve of her, and trace it and lick it and suck those places until they are pink from my efforts.

I make her come.

I make her come again, then again, then again, so many times that she weeps with pleasure.

Still, I'm not sated.

I still want more of her.

My cock stays hard and throbbing and insistent. Too insistent to turn over and sleep. Far too insistent to pretend I can ignore it. My life has waited for her. For this moment. I need nothing else.

In an instant, as the feeling overwhelms me, I flip Idalis over onto all fours. With her on her belly, her head on one of the pillows, her hips lifted toward me. I nudge the head of my cock into her opening while playing with her clit and she lets out a long, quiet moan. *Fucking perfect.*

She is open for me, and ready, and I enter her again with a deep thrust. I love the way she grips the sheets and how her swollen lips part with my name.

Gripping her hips, I hold her in place. Idalis only rocks her hips a little, taking me deeper.

"Do not move," I order. "Stay here. I need you to stay here."

"Yes," she breathes. "Yes."

Her pussy clenches around me, hot and tight and slick with both of us, and I drop my head back and release a low growl into the air. I do not know what to do with the sensation that overwhelms me. I do not know how to handle so much pleasure. I have handled pain many times, but this is so much more intense that it turns my thoughts to mud.

It's a deep need that I cannot fight.

I curl back toward her and bend my head, folding forward to cover her. Idalis spreads her thighs wider to accommodate me, but she does not need to. I am already seated inside her, and she was made to take me.

My cock pulses inside her.

I balance myself over her, rolling my hips only because I must move, I must *do* something to handle this pleasure. I breathe deeper, my blunt nails digging into her skin.

Fuck, she's gorgeous like this. Her hair is a mess and yet perfect. I can only see half her face, but the cheek visible to me is flushed pink. Her lips are slightly parted, and there's a small curve to her lips.

"I need to claim you," I tell her, and kiss the nape of her neck.

Idalis did not ask to be my mate. There was no way she could have predicted this would happen. We were brought together by fate.

She would probably say it was her spell that brought us here, not fate, but couldn't fate have guided her hands?

Moving her hair to the side, she offers me her neck. "Claim me."

I react instantly, biting her neck just enough to break skin and as I do, I fuck her recklessly. Forcing pleasure over her body as she cries out. The bed pounds against the wall as I lick and kiss the wound. My hips piston as the pleasure builds and I chase my climax.

Finally we come together, and I've never felt so complete.

Idalis lets me go with a soft sigh and turns into my arms when I lay on the pillow. She fits her body to mine and adjusts her head on my chest.

Her heart pounds. It takes a while for it to settle, as if she is waiting for me to give chase or go into battle with her or initiate another round. When her fingertips touch the mark, that's already started to heal from my licks, she smiles. A faint beautiful smile. My heart swells.

My world revels in the fact that my mate is here. She's safe in my arms, and has been pleasured to the very limits of her body. There is no threat outside the cottage. There is no threat for miles. I do not know another place where we could have such complete solitude, though that makes me ache for her as well. A woman like Idalis should not have had to keep herself so secluded.

We stay tangled in the sheets for a long time, avoiding the rest of the world. When goosebumps cover Idalis's shoulder, I tug the blankets up and make sure she is well covered, but first I plant on a kiss on her bare skin. It's a sin to cover her. I crave her skin against mine for as long as I can have it. Until dawn. Until the next day. Until...until I'm forced to go back.

As quickly as I can, I force that thought to fade away. I wish I could stay right here for years, but it's not possible for a soldier. I'll allow myself the fantasy a little longer. As her soft hums surround me with tender touches, I do everything I can not to think of what will come.

It's dark in the cottage, and the sounds outside

are those of the deep part of the night. I drift in the peace of the moment, entranced with the softness of Idalis's skin and the warmth of her body in my arms. She's not yet fallen asleep and makes no move to get up. I wonder if her thoughts are where mine are. If she has the same feelings I do, even though she's not a wolf. So many thoughts race in my mind and yet I feel peace with her. Comfort and peace. She lies there with her hair spilling over my chest as I let my fingers slip over her curves. After a while, I thread my fingers through her hair, inhaling the scent of her.

This is how it should be.

She doesn't seem shocked to find herself as my mate. She doesn't ask questions. I wonder how much my little witch knows. Perhaps she sensed something in the air the moment our eyes met.

I lose myself in her smallest movements. Every breath she takes. The soft touch of her fingertips on my chest. The heat underneath her palms.

As my head clears from the rush of such intense mating, another desire rises in me.

To allow her to see the parts of me I have guarded for most of my life. It was known in my pack. It was known to some in the army. But someone like Idalis?

I've never shared this with someone like her. And it's clear to me that I should share now. Before the hours tick on. She needs to know of the curse.

"I wasn't supposed to have a mate." My voice is more hoarse from the long silence than I anticipated. I clear my throat and peek down at her. Her gaze holds nothing but kindness and understanding. No shock. No judgment.

A weight lifts off me. As she licks her bottom lip, preparing to speak, Idalis repositions her head on my chest.

"You were not?" she asks, softly, as if she does not want to wake me from the spell of the night. She traces another circle on my chest. "Do not all shifters have mates? You didn't know you'd find me one day?"

With my eyes closed, it could almost be that night again, with the troll who told me I was cursed. Her eyes had burned with a strange light, and I didn't want her to tell me of my fate. She told me anyway. The words from her lips turned the world dark and empty around me. What she said stripped me of any future I might have hoped for and left me to bear the burden in the privacy of my own mind. I wanted to close my eyes so she could not look into them, but I could not bring myself to do it.

It was a warm night in midsummer until she spoke. Then it was as cold as the dead of winter. Alone in the woods in my teenage years, I'd stumbled upon her. Fear struck me first, but I could have never imagined what she would prophesize.

For years after that, I suffered, hiding it as well as I could. I was angry and resentful, and I couldn't understand why the troll had done it to me. Of all my pack, I was destined to be alone and they knew it. Never to have purpose or love.

Guilt consumed me whenever I had those thoughts. With every season that passed, the anger inside me burned hotter and hotter until it threatened to burn every relationship I had to the ground.

The day the last of my brothers found his mate, I left the pack.

It was painful, to be so alone, but not as painful as being surrounded by all of them with their mates. I was alone until I joined the army, but even then I was separated from the rest of my comrades by the curse. Even those who knew nothing about it seemed almost untouchable. It was pointless to form too many bonds with the other soldiers because we would live lives with nothing in common.

They would have wives or mates and families.

I would have myself. For all eternity alone. And

so I became the best that I could be in combat. The strongest. The most fearless. After all, if someone were to sacrifice themselves, it should be me. I have less to lose.

"I was cursed," I say, and more weight disappears. I had not known it was so heavy. "I was told that I would never mate with a wolf. A troll told me decades ago."

There is a short pause as Idalis absorbs my words.

"That…does not sound like a curse to me," she ventures. "It was a prophecy meant to shape you into who you are, perhaps."

"It seemed like a curse at the time. I believed I would spend the rest of my life alone." I stare at the ceiling as the pain ripples through me and the years of mourning flash in my mind. "I told myself I was dealing with it, but all I was doing was burying any feelings I had so they could not tear me apart. But I had to make difficult choices to do that. I had to leave my pack."

Idalis stiffens. "They did not accept you once you had been cursed?"

"No, they did. They never turned their backs on me. But eventually, I had to turn my back on them. It was tearing me apart to watch them find their mates and begin their lives when I would never do the same. It's been years since I've had a pack. Years since I've seen my family."

It'd always been so joyous for everyone when a member of the pack found a mate. It was only a reminder of my loneliness, no matter how much I tried to deny it. No matter how I attempted to hide the pain, it was always there, consuming me from the inside out.

Their excitement and passion swept through the whole pack. We would shift and hunt, howling our gratitude to the moon. I hated every moment of it. I hated how much I despised those celebrations. I wanted nothing more than to be happy for my brothers, but I couldn't be. I was too jealous.

All those celebrations only served to remind me of what I was forbidden to have.

"When there was no other wolf without a mate, I set out by myself," I whisper into Idalis's hair, still unable to look her in the eyes. "I left."

My voice breaks on the final word, and I bury my face in her hair.

Slipping her arm around my waist, Idalis holds me tighter. Her warmth and comfort soothe the brokenness inside of me. Her heartache and empathy thicken the air, but her pain and mine are eased by the bond between us.

It's so strong and soothing that it washes away some of the worst pain I have carried with me. Like a spell of its own. Every breath Idalis takes seems to draw more of it away.

"I'm sorry, Ryker," she says after a long while.

"There is nothing to apologize for."

She lifts her head to look at me, her hand on my chin, forcing me to meet her beautiful gaze. "I can't change what happened, but I can be sorry nonetheless. You shouldn't have had to go through that. It must've been terrible to spend all that time thinking you would remain alone." Another long pause. "I... know how it is." Her tone lowers capturing my full attention. She has a confession of her own. "My coven also left." She swallows thickly. "They're gone forever." Her voice cracks, tears pricking her eyes. "And I could not see any other way to live than by staying here, alone."

"I'm sorry." I offer her my condolences and gently kiss her on the lips.

I hold her closer. "I had given up."

"I had given up, too," Idalis admits with a quiet laugh. "I thought I was content here until you came." A simper slips onto her full lips. "Until you came, my fated wolf." She caresses my jaw. "Even my cards didn't see you coming."

A candle burns to life nearby, lending us enough light that I can see her eyes spark with a delight I'd not seen yet. She is perfect. Soft. Lush. Like I imagined my mate would be, only better, because I had never imagined a woman like Idalis.

I pull her up from the pillow and run my fingers through her hair, then hold her face in my hands. There is one part of the future that I find I cannot ignore, no matter how much I want to. I would rather ignore it as long as possible, but this moment demands honesty.

"I will have to leave you," I murmur. "To fight in the war."

Idalis's smile falters. "That is what my coven did. They believed some of us must fight in the war. We all did. But none of them returned with me. I watched them all die in the fire on the battlefield."

Without knowing what to say, I can only hold her tighter. The tragedy of war keeps my throat tight, and my words choke me.

Idalis looks into my eyes in the faint candlelight. "What if I said I didn't want you to go?"

Ryker looks deeply into my eyes, as if he is letting my words sink in slowly. I feel selfish even asking. I know he must. I only wish it were not so soon. I've only just met the love of my life, and I don't think I could bear to part from him.

His fingers are still in my hair when he kisses me again, slower than before. It's a very tender kiss in comparison to the wild way he has taken me for the past stretch of time. Has it been hours? It seems as if it must have taken at least that long, though it also seems like no time at all.

I sink into the kiss, my heart aching from the question I have asked.

What if I said I did not want you to go?

What if? *What if?* What would happen if I meant

it with all my heart? What would happen if he agreed to stay here instead of returning to his post as a soldier? In his kiss, I feel a world of possibilities open before me. It is like finding new moons in the sky that I have looked at for all these years. Like maybe it's possible.

It came upon me so fast—the thought that I might want him here with me. It's something I never thought I would admit to anyone in the world. There was never any reason to think I would have anyone again, because the risk to my heart is too great. I have lost so much. I know how reckless it is to give up my heart once again.

Yet I cannot help it. There is an undeniable pull to him.

If Ryker were to leave and I were to remain silent —if he left without knowing how much I wanted him—then I know I would regret my silence for the rest of my life.

I had to ask. And I am done regretting. I've spent years regretting that I did not perish with my coven and trying to cover that regret of staying back to aid a fallen soldier with the thought that I loved solitude.

In some ways, yes, I did love being alone. Having time to heal and mourn and allow my powers to be felt by all who needed it. The peace I found in my fields and with my gardens was real. It simply wasn't…complete.

Ryker groans softly against my lips, and another wave of hope comes over me. It's matched with a wave of desire that should be impossible, given how much we have already had each other.

But then—I've heard that mates who are fated to be together have periods of time like this, when they can crave each other for hours. Days, even. Getting lost in the depths of pleasure and desire with one another.

I feel as if I have craved Ryker all my life.

And perhaps that is why I have survived. Perhaps that is why I have lived. It's such a simple thing, to have a craving satisfied. To taste something so sweet.

I'm not satisfied quite yet.

As my fingers curl and I fist the sheets beside us, I know I need more of Ryker.

He pushes me down onto the pillows, covering me with just as much hunger as he had before, his cock hard and the rest of his muscles bunching with his need.

Could I even watch him leave, after having experienced this feeling?

I've spent so much time asking the moon for

answers. Begging her to reassure me in the only purpose I had left without my coven. Begging her to satisfy me with the peace of the valley and the good I did for the villagers who write to me for spells.

If I were to follow him…the thought slips into the back of my mind. To finish what my coven started.

It would be a loss to my land. The villagers would lose the magic of the spells. There would be a void left in my place. My mind whirls to fields that never have felt my footsteps or my magic.

In the dream I woke from, I *knew* that land. I knew it so well, though the fields were not the ones I have dwelled in. My heart races with possibility.

If that was a vision, or a prophecy…

Then those new lands would know my coven through me. I would carry their memory into my new life. Their magic, their power, our ways which would be lost had I not carried on.

I would *have* a new life. A new beginning of adventure. Although the very idea brings an anxiousness to me that's dangerous.

I cannot think much more about following that path, because Ryker kisses me even deeper, his hand coming up to brace my jaw as his cock presses into me and desire burns hotter between us. From the corner of my eye, I notice more candles illuminate around us, guided by my magic to give me just enough light to look into his eyes. He pulls back, kisses me again, then watches my face with deep intent as his hands roam my body, rediscovering places he has touched before and worshipping them just the same.

My nipples harden, my eyes go half lidded and I nearly fall victim to another climax simply watching his eyes heat as he toys with me.

He gradually slips his fingers across my needy pussy and searches out my clit, then watches from only inches away as he coaxes another orgasm from me. They take less time to arrive now, but they also take longer to melt away. Each one building on the last. My back arches as I cry out his name, my nails scratching down his back gently. My pleasure only fuels him. Ryker seems fascinated by this. He draws out a second, then a third, and I put my hand on his wrist, gasping.

I will light this cottage on fire if I come again. I am sure of it.

"A moment," I whisper, my eyes closed as heat travels up my chest and neck all the way up my face to my temple. My body rages with both heat and pleasure. "Only a moment."

Ryker presses his lips against my neck, his breath sending more warmth through my body making my toes curl. I'd thought I had reached an impossible peak—one I might not be able to come down from— but the intensity of the pleasure ebbs until I can bear it again.

Until I find myself wanting more.

I turn my face to Ryker's and find his lips with mine.

"Idalis," he says into my mouth. "My *Idalis*."

When I reach for him, he understands instantly what I want and lifts me onto his lap, straddling him. As if reading my mind. The cool air on my skin makes my nipples tighten and Ryker notices, teasing one of them with his thumb. Playing with my body and I love it. His cock is hard and thick underneath me, and his other hand comes to my waist.

I love his steady touch. I love the look in his eyes. I love how his breathing gets heavier.

His eyes stay on mine, though his breathing gets ragged as I lower myself until my opening is poised over the thick head of his cock.

Then I sink down, slowly taking him in. My eyes close slowly, savoring every second of this moment.

Ryker lets his head fall back to the headboard and

groans. I've never seen something so fucking sexy in my life as him lost in our touch.

It's my turn to treasure the look on his face as I lower myself, guiding him inch by throbbing inch into the heat of my body.

As I work myself onto his cock, he twitches inside me, his hand flexing on my waist. His other hand drops to my other hip, and he steadies me, letting me drag out the last few inches until I am fully seated. Filled and wanting.

My head falls back, and I moan as my body adjusts to the final stretch. How can it be that he fits me so perfectly, yet still stretches me?

A thrill shivers down my spine. Ryker is not the only one with a fated mate. *I* have one as well. The giddy joy of it is far stronger than I had ever guessed it would be, and it heightens yet another wave of pleasure.

I have him now. He is just as much mine as I am his. A lover. A hope of more in this life. All the twists and turns have led me to him. All the things I did to protect myself guaranteed that he could reach me.

Ryker wraps me in his arms and guides me over his cock, letting out quiet grunts and heated curses through clenched teeth. We've been wrapped in each other for hours, yet every motion feels new and addictive.

Not even my powers are enough to keep my knees from shaking. As I climb higher and higher, Ryker rolls us over so that he is propped above me, his cock buried deep. He ravages me, taking control and pistoning his hips as if he needs me to scream out his name in pleasure more than anything else. Which is exactly what I do and he rides out my orgasm, but slows before his own is found. With gentle kisses on my jawline, I press my head into the pillow, desperate for air so I can breathe.

He pulls his hips back, a long, slow slide that makes me gasp, and thrusts back in. Then he sets a rhythm that's steady and deep and fills me completely with each stroke. His lips part and he huffs out short breaths, but he never takes his eyes from my face. I want to see him like this in every part of life. There is so much intensity in him to match his soldier's strength, and when it is all focused on me, it's the only thing I want in the world.

His kisses are deep and include a few nips of my bottom lip. It seems he will never be satisfied that I have had enough pleasure, because he makes me come again with his fingers, and then again with just the angle of his hips.

Delirious with pleasure, I fall apart on the sheets, gasping and crying out and trembling. Ryker switches to making me come *gently*, which I had not thought was something that he could do after I had come so many times, but he can do anything.

I can do anything with him.

This is a form of magic. This pleasure and union. It's strong and this spell will never be broken. I come again just from that thought, and Ryker growls into my ear, speeding up his thrusts.

It feels as if it's healing the broken parts of me and doubling my powers and clearing my head all at once. This has to be fate. It has to be a sign from the moon.

As another orgasm threatens, I cry out, clutching at Ryker, begging even though I can hardly form words. I know it will not make sense to him. It does not even make sense to me. But I want him to stay. I want him inside me. I want him to be *with me*, no matter what happens.

Ryker answers with his body. He pumps deeper inside me, thrusting with so much power that he can hardly find my lips with his. He manages it every so often, and we press open-mouthed kisses to each other's lips. It's sinful and everything I need right now.

I spread my thighs wider and hook my legs behind his back, and then I have no choice but to fall off the edge of a forbidden cliff on the all-consuming pleasure of him.

He fucks deep into me and roars out his pleasure as he comes deep inside of me.

We fall to the pillows after that, and Ryker throws his arm over me. For a while, there is no sound but our heavy breathing.

As sleep drifts into my mind's eye, I don't think I could get up to go to the window and search for the moon, but I do not need to. The moon is always there.

I close my eyes and picture her in the sky.

Please, I think, with my heart as open as it has ever been. *Let me have this love in all that it can be. Please, let him stay with me. I want our broken souls to heal each other. He is already healing mine. Please.*

I take a few deep breaths.

"So mote it be," I whisper to the moon. "So mote it be."

I am still whispering it as I fall asleep.

Sweet Dreams Spell Jar

To SLEEP WITH PEACE, deeply and easily gather the following items:

A JAR TO hold the spell, but it must have a lid
    Blue celestite chips for sleep
    Dried chamomile for peace
    Rosemary for focus
    Jasmine for waking happily and rested
    A little sugar for sweet dreams

ADD each ingredient in the order above. As you add them make sure you tell each item their purpose. Then light a soft blue or white candle and seal your jar.

SLEEP WELL, sleep deep. Those sweet dreams are for you to keep.
    So mote it be.

I didn't doubt that Idalis was my mate. It's not the kind of knowledge that can be doubted. Not the kind of feeling that can be second-guessed for long. It's far above the level of thought.

But if I had doubted, all of those doubts would have disappeared as she came for me, over and over again, and *with* me, staring into my eyes as if she had never seen anything more intriguing or precious.

When I finally come inside her one final time and find myself dragged down to the depths of a peaceful sleep, I have the feeling the night will last forever. It's as if the moon has stopped time for us, and I don't need to worry about the sunrise, or the following days, or my place in the army waiting for me even now.

I don't have to worry about anything.

I'm no longer cursed, and I'm no longer alone. For the first time, I close my eyes in a perfect world. Idalis lies next to me, her heart beating fast but settling slowly as sleep takes her under as well.

I would linger in this night forever if fate would let us.

Instead I sleep, deep and dreamless, somehow aware of her next to me. My wolf reaching out for her every so often to be sure my mate is safe and sound.

She is. She will always be safe beside me. Time has made me a great warrior and perhaps that's what I needed to be so I could live up to be fated to the powerful witch.

I've a few shallow dreams that are mostly fragments. Sounds and scents. Memories of Idalis in the candlelight above me and under me, the tiny flames reflecting in her gorgeous eyes.

The world has not been stopped by the moon after all. The night moves slowly through its remaining hours. I don't care about the world outside the cottage, but my wolf has an understanding that is rooted deeper into the ground, and he keeps watch, as he always has.

I wake slowly wishing a new day would hold off.

The gods could not stop the new day from coming, but it is waking up slowly as well. The sunlight that caresses Idalis's windows is gentle. It is early yet.

Idalis sleeps deeply in my arms, her breathing slow and steady. There is no worry in her. No tensions. She's let all her weight fall onto me in the night.

For a while, I simply lie there, savoring the moment. My mate. My beautiful and powerful mate. How have I gotten so lucky?

Many men have trusted me with their lives during my time in the army. I've taken that trust as the sacred bond that it was. I didn't think I would experience a bond more sacred. I would have sworn there would never be one.

Yet, here we are and here it is.

I watch the light grow bit by bit. No one comes to drag me from the bed. There are no sounds of the army preparing for the day around me. Nothing *compels* me to ease Idalis out of my arms and leave her behind.

Not yet.

I savor that, too. There were no shouts to rouse me from my sleep. There were no war horns or drums. Idalis asleep in my arms is the greatest peace I have ever known.

No more prophecy. No more curse. They are both broken, both dissolving into the past like they never existed. From this day forward, I am free of that sorrow. Although now another persists. I must leave her. After the royal wedding, we return to the battlefield. War does not wait for love.

I don't allow myself to think that another sorrow will come to replace it. For now, there's no such thing.

Eventually, a soft sound gets my attention. At first it is like the chirping of an insect outside the cottage, but the more I listen for it, the more familiar it becomes.

One of my crystals.

Idalis doesn't stir from the sound. Carefully, I move her gently to the pillows and cover her with the blankets. She turns over with a sigh and continues sleeping, nestled into the warmth of the bed.

I find a pair of pants and a shirt, then go to my pack and draw out the crystals. The morning sun is brighter when I leave the cottage and find Idalis's small outdoor table.

I'm sure it is Jorge who is trying to summon me. Adrenaline rushes in my blood at the thought. My mouth goes dry with nervousness.

When the call connects, I'm proven right.

"Ryker," my commander says. "Can you hear me? It seems the storm has passed."

There's a note of optimism in his voice that makes my heart ache. Jorge is the person who is most like my brothers. I'd protect him as if he were a member of my pack, and he would protect me just the same. We've seen horrors together. Survived together and conquered together.

"I can hear you," I answer him. The morning breeze ruffles my hair. It is already warm. The storm has passed. The day will be a lovely one. It reassures me that Idalis won't hear this conversation even if she wakes. A twinge of nervousness prickles through me at that idea, and another at the idea that Jorge might give me news that shatters the peace I've only just found.

"I've received word that the portals across Athica are working again." Jorge doesn't smile as he says this. His expression remains serious, though not frustrated, and I ache again at how familiar he is to me. "Have you tested them yourself?"

"Not yet," I answer. "I've only just woken." His brow arches at that information. "I've news as well." My pulse quickens as I shift where I sit. Unsure of how he will take the news.

"What news?" Jorge questions, his brow slightly raised.

I answer him as quickly as the words will leave me. "I've found my mate."

With wide eyes, he stares back incredulously. He blinks several times. "Shifters? In the witch's territory?"

"No." My throat goes tight at the admission I'm about to make. "The witch herself. Idalis is my mate." A longing possesses me that I didn't know I'd feel. His acceptance means more to me than I anticipated. His happiness for my union. It's as if the guilt of all of the years of jealousy and denial weigh down in this moment, finding my mating undeserving. As if it's a lie. As if it cannot be because she is not wolf.

Stunned, Jorge takes a moment to correct his expression. He's silent for a moment and I half expect for his image to fade from the crystal, and for the connection to have broken. Perhaps broken purposefully.

Finally, Jorge shakes his head as if composing his thoughts. He clears his throat before straightening his shoulders to speak.

"You have fought for decades beside me," he says, his voice rough.

"I know." The years go by in my memory as a collection of colors and marches and battles. Of blood on claws and Jorge's face dirty from the fight and his hand clasping my shoulder. "Commander, I—"

He interrupts me with a stern tone. "You've been by my side while other men have come and gone. When their families needed them. When their lives changed."

"I have," I agree and nod.

"I grant you leave," Jorge says, and I'm stunned at how easily it rolls off his tongue. With a pull to his lips and a softness to his eyes, he speaks with compassion and understanding.

My throat goes tight. I hadn't even thought to request it.

"You will spend as much time with your mate as you need. You have both served and seen more than your share of what war brings."

"If the war changes, and if you need me, I will return. I will fight beside you. I made an oath, and I will keep it."

Jorge smiles, and it is the smile he has given other men—a smile of genuine congratulations. There is no jealousy in it, and no sense that he thinks I am abandoning my duties. It is simple happiness from a friend, and I return it to him. Grateful more than anything.

"I have received your message," Jorge says. "I'll file the paperwork, Ryker. Congratulations."

"Thank you."

"You will attend the wedding still?" he questions with uncertainty. "Perhaps there is a way she could aid us with you beside her... I'd like to meet her, if you could convince her to attend."

With the early morning light slipping into the cottage, I wake deeply rested—though with my muscles still aching, especially between my thighs. I take a few minutes letting myself get used to the day. A smile finds its way to my lips. It doesn't feel real. I've found love. Well I suppose love has found me. With that thought, I peer down to the pillow beside me.

Ryker's not in the bed with me. Patting the sheet next to me, I find it cool to the touch.

I can sense, somehow, that he has not gone far. Is that because of a bond we've created between us? I think it must be. Delight fills me with warmth. A new kind of magic exists. A kind I can play with for the first time.

If only he can stay as I asked. At least for a little while.

Although he didn't say he would or that he could. Ryker answered in kisses and touches and his body, but we didn't stay awake long enough after that final round to have a deeper conversation. Tension strains my heart.

It's been so long since I have felt companionship and never did it feel like this. I fear losing it just as quickly as it's found me.

For all I did tell him, there's much I haven't said as well. I didn't tell him that I don't think I can bear such a loss a second time.

Here in my bed, with the scent of him still on the sheets, it's hard not to let my thoughts turn toward him completely. It's true that we haven't known each other for long, but he is my *mate*. I know the heart of him. And I know that he is a highly trained weapon. He has spent his life building himself into the best soldier he could be.

I know the army has been his entire purpose. His entire life. He would be giving up all that once to stay with me. If they would allow it.

Was it right for me to propose such a thing?

It is too late to take back the words, even if I

wanted to, and I do not. As I always do, I drift toward thoughts of my books. Of the ancient grimoires for answers. But one thing resonates through me and keeps me still and at peace.

I was made for him.

I will be with him regardless. Always. We cannot be separated. This magic is impossible to break.

Whether it was the moon or simply fate itself, I was destined for Ryker. And he was destined for me.

With a deep breath in and a slow breath out, I release all those worries and thoughts to the moon. The moon might not be as visible, but she is still there in the sky. She is always there to hold the burdens I cannot carry alone.

Spurred by my need to find him, I throw over the covers and I get out of bed. I imagine he's only gone for a quick run. I go to my bathing room and wash quickly, letting the water trickle down over my skin, treating myself gently. Reminding myself that I can survive anything and with this new love, so much more awaits.

As I wash the most tender parts of myself I blush. I've never given myself to a man before. I've heard of the pleasures, but I could have never know it would be so all-consuming and divine. I do wonder if being fated made it more intense or whether it's always like that.

My desire for Ryker hasn't waned at all. My clit is still sensitive although all of the rest of me is sore. I shiver as I pull a clean dress over my head, my skin even more sensitive to the fabric. It's been kissed and sucked and bitten now and carefully marked by my mate. My fingers drift to my neck finding a faint mark in the mirror. Only a slightly silver scar remains.

I love it.

I'm already at peace with that change. I do not see how it could be any other way. It's like being at peace with having a heart, or a soul. It is simply part of me.

I'm even at peace with this small interval of solitude while Ryker is outside. I know how to spend time alone. It's not at all the same as *being* alone for all these years, with only the letters with pleas for help and only the creatures of the forest for company. This is a solitude that knows it will soon be broken. That my mate is nearby and will return.

And that speaks to me to the depths of my soul. Selecting a simple crimson silk dress that falls down to the floor, I speak my intent for the day: *Passion and love will guide me today and I will trust in it. So mote it be.*

Those little bits of magic, simple statements of what you wish even in mundane acts like getting dressed or washing your face, that little bit of magic is so very powerful and should not be overlooked. I do them as often as I can and from now on they will include thoughts of Ryker.

My steps are sure as I select a candle from my shelf. Not the candle I burned for my spell, of course, because that one has nothing more to give. Perhaps the spell went as wild as it did because I was trying to give the prince and princess something I wanted desperately for myself but believed I would never have.

Somehow, my powers turned those words into *Ryker.* The spell did not create him, but it did create the situation that allowed us to discover one another. For fate to finally bring us together as we were meant to be.

So...was it a mistake that led to a violent storm and trapped him here, or something else? I wished for no harm to come if I didn't attend to the wedding. If he wasn't trapped here, Ryker may have never found me. Unless we'd both attended the wedding. What could have been is not mine to see, but I am grateful for what I have been given, including spells gone awry.

Is it ever a mistake if all a witch is doing is guiding herself onto fate's path?

I cannot say.

I bring the candle to my worktable and sit down with it.

I close my eyes, reach for the comfort of the moon, and focus on a spell of truth. Not a spell of prophecy. Not a spell of comfort. Not a spell that will tell me what I want to hear.

A spell that will tell me what *is* and what will be.

I etch the words into the candle, murmuring them softly and holding myself and Ryker in my mind. I'm careful not to place us anywhere in particular. I do not want to influence the spell in that way. It's just the two of us, the background indistinct. The only important aspect is him, not *where*.

It's difficult, I will admit, not to influence the spell, but I remain strong, to manifest what I desire rather than to pray for our highest selves to be shown.

The moon *must* have a reason for all this. She must.

I search the candle flames. For a minute, there is nothing.

Then it dances slightly differently, and the world around me dims. It doesn't go so dark that it disappears, more so to alert me that it is not the time to look at the present. It is time to look upon the future the spell has shown me.

The first clear image to appear is me, and a second later, Ryker. He stays beside me until we are both old and gray. The sight of us together, knowing we make it many moons together, brings me such comfort the back of my eyes prick with tears. I don't wish to be alone anymore. I only wish to be with him.

The image shifts, seeming to move backward in time, whirling through different vibrant colors as it does. There we are again, much younger than we eventually became but slightly changed from how we are now. Pups play in the grass in the background. In the distance, those pups tumble and chase until they at last grow older and become wolves and among them a young witch playing with fire. She has Ryker's eyes.

The seasons change, too. This is more a feeling than an image, but I understand with perfect clarity.

There is a hand on my shoulder.

I keep my mind focused on the images brought to

me by my spell. It is the truth without a doubt. This is what we will be.

This is where the future begins.

He is quiet in the present, letting me watch.

"What do you see?" he asks eventually.

My heart swells with this new truth. "I see that you love me forever."

"I already knew I'd do that," he says softly behind me, planting a kiss on the crook of my neck.

I let out a sob that's half a laugh and turn away from the future. It's a seed I have planted, only it's one that I cannot hurry to grow faster. It will bloom in its own time. And what must come, will. But I have comfort in the love we have today.

I stand up and the tiniest movement brings me into Ryker's arms. He tips my face to his. Giddy nervousness overtakes me. "I don't know what's going to happen exactly or how we will get there, but—"

He smiles at me. "Step by step, I would think."

A huff of a laugh leaves me at his statement. "Can we start with getting to know each other?"

"We did last night," he teases, and another laugh escapes me.

"We have forever but I want it all now," I tell him

truly. "I want to know everything there is about you."

Ryker thinks about it for a moment. "I'll start. My favorite season is summer."

I don't think I could smile any wider at his admission. "Mine is winter. And—" I search for a truth about myself. "Lillies make me sneeze but I think they're beautiful."

"What's your favorite flower then?" he asks.

"What's yours?" I counter.

"The tropical ones, like birds-of-paradise."

"I love peonies and roses."

"Then I will build you a rose garden," he tells me. *Where?* The question hisses in the back of my mind but I don't speak it. Instead I tell him another truth of mine.

"The outside world is dangerous, and it's scared me for years now."

He touches my face with a fondness, staring deep into my eyes. He leans forward as if he'll kiss me but instead he whispers, "The outside world is beautiful and thrilling."

My heart beats faster, knowing he's right, knowing I will venture to places I haven't known but that he'll be beside me.

Ryker's eyes flash with a knowing desire. "This all happened for a reason."

"What reason?" I question wondering why fate had us meet this way. *Why now?*

"This reason." He kisses me with a passion that weakens my knees. It doesn't matter that he had me over and over last night. It doesn't matter at all. I kiss him back as fiercely as I ever have, and Ryker sweeps me into his arms and presses me back against the wall in a few hurried strides.

I'm drowning in desire by the time his cock is hard against my hip. I writhe against him needing to have him inside of me again.

Lifting me by my hips, with my legs wrapped around his waist, Ryker fucks me up against the wall, uninhibited and free, and the push of him inside me and his hard body in front of me can be nothing but heaven. I clench around him, pleasure building in me until I come undone. Once? Twice? I lose track in our touch and the heated kisses. In his primal need. And Ryker follows me, thrusting hard inside me until he kisses me one more time before he finds his own climax.

He leans his forehead against mine, my body still wrapped around his, and catches his breath. Then he kisses my cheek and then nips the lobe of my ear.

With his lips at the shell of my ear, his warm breath sends shivers down my shoulders. "You don't have to ever question that I am yours or whether I'll ever come back to you," he says, and then pulls back so I can look into his eyes.

His eyes have never seemed brighter or more possessive. They have never seemed more wolf-like. But I know it is him I am seeing.

I am seeing his very soul.

"Fate brought us together," he continues. "Not your spell."

"Fate *and* my spell brought us together," I correct, playing one last round of our game. He lets out a huff of a laugh at my correction, giving into me.

"I love you, Idalis," he whispers. "My soul was meant to be with yours."

I'm filled with so much joy that I can hardly breathe, but then I must, because here is my new life and my mate, before me at last.

"I took some pleasure in my solitude," I begin, then pause, choked with emotion. "But I did feel sorrow. I told myself that I didn't long for anything. That I was content with my purpose. I told myself it would be safer to be alone. But then you stepped onto my land, and into my life, and I knew *longing*. I never knew longing like that until you looked at me.

I love you Ryker. And there is no doubt that I will love you forever."

A Spell for a Happily Ever After

FOR A HAPPILY EVER AFTER, I suggest the following be placed in a red, pink, or white satchel cleansed by sitting in pink salt overnight before adding your ingredients and tucking it away under the bed you share with your lover.

ROSE PETALS for passion
 Rose quartz for love
 Clear quartz for longevity
 Lavender for peace in union
 Obsidian chips for protection
 Dried wine stained on the tip of a cork from a shared bottle (the cork could be added whole if preferred and if there is room) for divine blessing
 A parchment with both of your names, folded three times toward you before being slipped into the satchel.

Do not worry if the parchment folds come undone, the spell has already been cast.

May your life be filled with love that is all-consuming. Love that never drifts. Love that you are so very worthy of. Know that you can have this love alone, as you should always love yourself fiercely. Or you can share the power of such divine emotion and magic with whomever you wish.

WITH ALL MY HEART, so mote it be.

RYKER

What will come, I don't know.

Whether I will return to the battlefield or whether war will end.

Whether I'll have to leave my mate or whether she will come with me.

But what I do know is that this moment is one I never thought I would have, let alone one I could dream.

And I will cherish it as every love should be cherished.

With cheers and loud masses, the wedding celebration spills outside the city gates. Banners fly on the city walls, their colors bright and fresh in the sun. People of all walks of life have come from miles and miles away. From different lands and of all ages. It's as if a new city has sprung up outside the walls, filling in every blank space in the small villages that already huddle close to the city.

There are hundreds of tents and wagons and firepits. Pots and pans clang and merchants shout about their wares, so many voices that it's hard to make out what they're saying.

Everything is loud and bright for the royal wedding. And hope is felt in every way for a new day.

It's made even louder and brighter from the time I spent in the solitude of the country with Idalis. The celebration and bustle is exhilarating. There is only happiness, made even greater with Idalis at my side.

She clings to me. Stoic with her draped hooded dress. It's thin but a dark crimson, which complements her pale skin, allowing her to see but hiding her all the same. She's lovely even if she attempts to hide. I heard her cast her spell for protection and for only blessings upon blessings for today. With her hand in mind, I am sure that is what the day will bring.

I take in the banners and tents and crowded streets. All the excited onlookers milling everywhere. Children running and playing games. Men and women laughing together.

And, for the first time...I think of my own wedding. Glancing down at my mate, I wonder if she will want one. I wouldn't have a wedding so large. My wedding, I think, would be suited to me and Idalis. A gathering of our closest friends, perhaps, in the rolling fields near her home. Dinner and dancing afterward. We would not draw crowds like this, and for that I am glad.

My friends will love her. She's a vision in her gown that flows down to her feet. My pack...when I see them again, will love her as well. That time will come soon as I've written to let them know that I have found a mate. My throat tightens as emotions overwhelm me, and I push them down. Everything will come in time, that I am sure of.

Idalis looks around, wide-eyed, at the joyful chaos around us, her hair flowing down her back in curls and her cheeks pink with excitement. Although she may not want others to see her, she certainly enjoys seeing others.

It's been quite a long time since she was in a crowd of this size.

I let her take her fill. Then, when she bites her lip,

I pull her into my arms and hold her close. Nothing compares to her. Not the cities or the celebrations or the grand displays.

I know that she's nervous, because inside the city walls, there are more people waiting for us. My commander Jorge. The prince and the princess… although I have been told something has changed. Many of my comrades.

"They will all love you," I promise her.

"I'm the witch who is so frightening she must live alone. So powerful she should be feared." She smiles, letting out a nervous laugh. Apprehension shines in her eyes.

"You don't live alone anymore," I point out. "And you are lovely. Many lovely people wish to live in solitude."

"Do they?" she teases. "Are you sure about that?"

"I have enjoyed my solitude with you."

She tips her face up to mine for a kiss. "Don't leave my side, please."

"I would never," I swear to her. "I love you."

"I love you too," Idalis answers.

She lifts herself on tiptoes for one more kiss before we step inside to join the celebrations.

The kiss seems to go on forever, and I wouldn't

mind if it did. It is a kiss shared with every part of me.

My soulmate.

My fated lover.

Mine forevermore.

My powerful little witch.

Thank you so much for reading my romances. I'm just a stay at home mom and avid reader turned author and I couldn't be happier.
I hope you love my books as much as I do!

To browse more of my books, visit https://willowwinterswrites.com/pages/reading-order

If you prefer *text alerts* so you don't miss any of my new releases, text
US residents: Text WILLOW to 797979
UK residents: Text WWINTERS to 82228